A Hairy Tail Collection

Also by the Author:

Ashes to Ashes

Gifted

Trouble

Dark Eyes: Cursed

Before The Fall

A World Without Angels

Angel's Uprising

Cinderella is Evil

Saving Rapunzel

Killing Snow White

A Hairy Tail Collection

JAMIE CAMPBELL

ISBN: 1492732303

ISBN-13: 978-1492732303

A Hairy Tail 1

Dedication

For Snoopy.

Chapter 1

Most people enjoyed their summer break. The sunshine, the beach, the cold drinks on a hot day, and, most importantly, not being at school. But not Hannah, she didn't find them interesting at all.

Of course, most people didn't enjoy school as much as she did. There was something about the buzz of getting things right, the way things were organized, and the idea you had to do something a certain way that just pleased her. It was everything else in the world that scared her. Unpredictability was a nightmare.

Hannah slumped on the chair, counting in her head how many days she had to wait for the chaos to be restored. Ninety-three, that's how many. She considered making a countdown calendar, that would take up a few minutes of her boring existence.

"You're not going to laze about here all summer." Her mother, the irrepressible Coco, butted into her thoughts. She stood over her, both hands on her hips, with that 'I'm not taking no for an answer' look on her face. Hannah hated that look.

"Well you wouldn't let me go to summer school, so what am I supposed to do?"

"Get a job, I don't care, just get out of this house. Be normal for once in your life and have some fun." Coco turned and left her there, letting her words sink into the seemingly impenetrable skull of her daughter.

Hannah waited just long enough for it not to be because she was told, to get up and do as she was told. She picked up her handbag and made a point of slamming the front door behind her.

So she was outside of the house, just like Coco ordered her. But now what? She looked from left to right at the other houses in the street. They were all exactly the same, two storey, shutters on the windows, friendly doormats on the porches. It seemed like the entire world was conforming and giving up on any hope of being an individual.

Hannah sighed and started walking. Mom said get a job, so she'd start there. At least when it all went wrong she would have someone to blame. Better than being accused of being lazy.

There were always jobs posted on the board outside the supermarket, Hannah had passed it thousands of times growing up. She never imagined she'd be using one of the ads to actually get employment, but there you go. Life was full of the unpredictable.

She stood in front of the board, searching for anything that appeared even remotely tolerable.

"I'm going to be a microbiologist and they expect me to have waitressing experience?" Hannah mumbled to herself.

If the jobs were menial, they required way more experience than she had. It seemed you either had to be a robot or a genius, there was nowhere in between where she could fall.

Buried underneath all the new advertisements, there was one faded sheet of paper. Hannah pulled it out, trying to work out what the words were. A large corner had been torn away, she had to fill in the blanks just to read it.

As she scanned the flyer, Hannah knew she had found her summer entertainment. The local animal shelter was looking for volunteers, apparently for a long time judging by the condition of the flyer. She carefully folded the piece of paper and started moving.

At fifteen years of age, her bicycle was the only form of transport she had – besides her feet anyway. She knew the streets of Mapleton like the back of her hand and able to fly along the roads without thinking twice.

Hannah had lived in the town since she was born. People rarely left the small county, preferring to make their way within the community. Hannah knew she would be different, she would happily leave one day to pursue her dream of being a scientist, they were rarely needed in Mapleton. She would come back to visit but that was it.

The Mapleton Animal Rescue Centre came into sight as she approached. Leaving her bike at the front gate, Hannah carefully entered, wondering if she had made the right decision or not. Animals weren't entirely her thing, she couldn't even remember why it had sounded so good in the first place. Perhaps it was the lack of customer service skills that it required.

"Can I help you?" The lady at counter asked, she seemed friendly enough. It helped calm her nerves slightly.

"I'm wondering if you still need volunteers?"

"Are you kidding, honey? We *always* need volunteers," she smiled an impossibly wide smile. "How old are you?"

"Fifteen."

"Can you work at least one four hour shift a week?"

"I can work every day over the summer."

"Can you speak cocker spaniel?"

Hannah was stumped, unsure if she was serious or not. That was the kind of unpredictable she feared. Still, the woman didn't seem like she was going to continue without an answer. "Um, I don't know, I've never tried. I'm smart, I'm sure I can learn it quickly."

The woman burst into laughter. "That was a joke, honey, but I like you. You're hired. You can start tomorrow, dress in something that can get dirty… and wet."

Hannah smiled, gulping at the same time. Either she had just made a huge mistake, or the best decision of her entire life. It could go either way.

Chapter 2

"These are the sponges, first you have to get them all wet and then rub in the shampoo," the manager, she had introduced herself as Cory, explained. "Then rinse them off again. Let them shake off the excess water and give them a rub down with the towel. Got it?"

Hannah seriously doubted whether she did indeed get it. "Got it."

"Good luck then." Cory left her in the room alone with nothing but a tub and a sponge. She didn't even have a clue where to start. When Cory asked Hannah if she wanted to get close and personal with the dogs, she didn't think she was being tricked into washing them.

Looking at the row of animals in their cages, Hannah questioned for the hundredth time whether she was doing the right thing. She didn't think it would be so sad seeing all the animals without homes.

But she had a job to do and unless she did it, she

would be there all day with her hands in warm water. She started with the smallest dog and worked her way up. After all, how much trouble could a little dog be?

Hannah soon found out. The little ones were wily and tricky, they were smart enough to avoid the sponge wherever they could. As it turned out, the bigger ones were much easier. They just stood there, unable to thrash about in the tub. Hannah made a mental note to keep her eyes on the small ones.

With one dog left, she stood in front of his cage. He was lying down, his head resting on his front paws. He didn't move to look at her, instead just his eyes lifted to meet hers. They were big and brown, but she didn't notice this at first. What Hannah saw was a painful sadness in his eyes.

"What's up, boy? You want a bath?"

He didn't move, just turned his eyes back to the floor again. She wasn't sure what breed he was, a little Labrador, a little Terrier, and perhaps a little German Shepherd. He didn't seem to be anything in particular – just depressed.

"A warm bath will make you feel better." She tried to sound excited but it wasn't convincing either of them. He could probably see how wet she was and sense it wasn't making *her* feel any better.

He wasn't budging. She carefully slid a hand underneath his belly and carried him over to the tub. He didn't argue or fight, he didn't even fidget. He just sat down in the water like he was pretending he was somewhere else.

Hannah sponged him carefully in case he was in any pain. He wasn't whimpering or anything, he just wasn't doing anything. It was weird, and she had to admit it made her a little uncomfortable.

"What's your story?" She asked him, never expecting an answer. It would have been cool though.

"He's been here for three months." The male voice came from behind, startling Hannah so much she threw the sponge into the air. It came down – right on top of her head. Soap and suds slowly started sliding down her face.

"Do you always sneak up on people?" She asked grumpily as she turned around. "It's not very-"

She stopped mid sentence as she saw who she was talking to. He was probably the cutest guy she had ever seen in her life – ever. His dark hair was thick with waves as it framed his gorgeous face. Setting it off were emerald green eyes that sparkled with his amusement. All the words suddenly fell right out of her head.

"Sorry, I didn't mean to scare you," he started. She instantly forgave him. "His name is Basil and he's been here for three months, that's his story."

She suddenly realized he was answering her question and she needed to say something too or she would look like an even bigger fool than she already did. "Oh. Three months? That's a long time, right?"

"Yeah, I think that's why he's so sad, nobody's claimed him yet. You must be new here, I'm Harry."

"Hannah. I started today."

"I can tell." He grinned.

"I wouldn't have thrown the sponge if you didn't sneak up on me," she pointed out, hating the way her face was burning with blushing.

"I just meant they always make the newbies wash the dogs. It's like an initiation ritual."

The burning was even worse now. Hannah doubted whether she would ever recover from the embarrassment. "Oh, right."

"Have fun," Harry said before walking backwards to sidle out the door.

Hannah let out the breath she was holding, wondering where her dignity had gone. The cutest guy on the planet and she had already made a fool of herself within ten seconds of meeting him. She deserved an award, it had to be a record.

She finished washing Basil and gave him extra attention when drying him. If he was lonely and missing his family, she wanted to at least let him know someone cared about him. If only she could get the dog to cheer up, his sad look was starting to get to her.

Cory returned to check on her progress. "All done?"

"Every single one of them. As you can see." She looked down at her soaking wet clothes. Every dog there had managed to spatter her with water. Plus the walls, the floor, and the windows too.

"Good job. Why don't you mop up this water and then play with the animals? You've earned some play time."

It sounded a lot easier than her first task. "Sure, I'd love to."

Hannah knew exactly which dog to start with. She quickly ran a mop over the floor and opened Basil's cage. Again, he didn't even begin to react. She picked him up and took him outside to the play area.

The area was really just a patch of grass with a fence around it, but it was outside in the sunshine and that had to make any dog happy. She placed him on the ground, making sure his four legs were holding his weight before letting go.

"Go for a run, Basil, go on," she urged. When he didn't move, she gave him a gentle nudge of encouragement. He took one step and stopped again.

She did the running for him, trying to get the dog to chase her. He reached almost up to her thigh so they couldn't run too far in the pen. Basil just stared at her like she was too much trouble.

Giving up, Hannah sat on the ground next to him. She put her arm right around his shoulders, bringing him in for a hug. Basil just let her, not doing anything to encourage or dissuade her.

"Someone will come and get you, Basil," she whispered.

Footsteps stomped behind her, Hannah looked around quickly and saw Harry standing there, waiting.

"I thought I would make sure you heard me coming this time, I wouldn't want you to accidently strangle Basil." His impossibly beautiful smile spread across his impossibly perfect lips.

"How kind of you," she replied sarcastically, trying to play it cool. The last thing she wanted to do was betray her fast-beating heart.

He sat on the other side of Basil, his hand absentmindedly stroking him. "He misses his family."

"I would too if I hadn't seen them in three months. Is he always this sad?"

Harry nodded. "Ever since he arrived. When he was found he was all thin and his hair was scraggly, he'd been out on his own for a while."

"He doesn't have a microchip or any identification? Something we can use to find his family?" Hannah figured they'd probably already done all they could, but had to ask anyway.

"He's an enigma. He wasn't wearing a collar and he's not microchipped. There's no way of telling where he has come from. Cory ran his picture in the paper a few times but nobody ever came forward."

"So how do you know his name?"

Harry held Basil's face in his hands, rubbing his ears. "Don't you think he looks like a Basil? I think he does."

Hannah couldn't argue, he *did* kind of look like a Basil. She couldn't see him as a Buster or Buddy or anything else more dog-like.

"So what's going to happen to him?" She asked, hoping for some good news.

"He needs to be adopted," Harry started. "But the problem is, he ignores anyone that looks at him. Everyone that wants to adopt just walks straight on by."

"He's waiting for his real family."

"I think he is," Harry replied. They both nodded in silence as Basil laid himself down, his head on his paws.

Chapter 3

"He's not on any of these ones either," Hannah sighed. She turned away from the message board and all the *Lost & Found* posters. A picture of Basil wasn't amongst them.

"Maybe he's not missing then," Veronica said. "Perhaps he was never owned by anyone in the first place?"

"He misses someone, he had to be part of a family."

"And you know this, how?"

Hannah shrugged. "I just know, okay? Maybe I'm psychic or something."

Veronica rolled her eyes but didn't say anything. They finally sat on the bench outside the supermarket in defeat. Hannah was all out of ideas. She couldn't get Basil's sad eyes out of her mind and it was driving her crazy. It was like having the pieces of a thousand piece jigsaw puzzle and not having the complete picture. In other words: Impossible.

Across the parking lot, Hannah spotted someone

waving. She looked at him, trying to focus across the distance. She realized it was Harry.

"Is that guy waving at us?" Veronica asked.

Hannah shyly waved back, feeling like an idiot for not seeing him sooner. "Yeah, but don't look at him."

"Why? He's cute. How do you know him?" She waved too, even though he wasn't paying any attention to her. She didn't notice.

"He volunteers at the shelter too, his name's Harry."

"Harry the hottie. Please tell me you've been flirting with him."

Hannah could feel the familiar heat crossing over her face as she blushed with the thought. "No, of course not. He wouldn't be into a girl like me. Guys that nice and good looking go for the popular girls. Not the nerdy, clumsy girls."

"There's no harm in a little flirting," Veronica replied resolutely. She was always trying to pull her best friend out of her shell but never really managed it.

"I don't even know how to flirt." Hannah stood, signaling the end of the conversation. Her love life, or lack of it, was not open for discussion. "Are you coming?"

"Fine." Veronica sighed as she followed.

They spent the rest of the afternoon at the beach. Hannah slathered herself in sunscreen and sat under the shade of an umbrella while Veronica basked in the sun in her bikini.

By the time evening rolled around, Hannah was glad to retreat back to her home. Veronica may be a great friend, but she was relentless in her attempts to get her to have fun.

"You're finally home, how was it at the shelter today?" Coco called from the kitchen. Hannah stopped, regretting not coming in through the back door.

"Fine."

Her mother leant against the kitchen door to speak with her, standing between her and the stairs. Hannah wasn't going to be able to pass without having a conversation.

"I'm pleased you're spending your time volunteering and helping the animals."

"Yeah, it's great." She made a move for the stairs but her mother wasn't quite done yet.

"I hope you realize that you need to do more than spend all your summer at the shelter." She scrutinized her daughter, searching for a reaction. "You need to spend time having fun too, socializing and enjoying being young. You're not going to be fifteen ever again, you do realize that, right?"

She couldn't help it, Hannah rolled her eyes. Perhaps Veronica would make a better daughter for Coco, they certainly had the same soundtrack. "I don't like going to parties, Mom, you should be happy about that."

"Normal teenagers go to parties, you should want to."

"What's so great about being normal?" Hannah stood there, waiting for an answer. Finally, Coco was lost for words.

Eventually, she replied. "Dinner is on in half an hour, go wash up."

Hannah smiled, one win for her, zero for her mother. It was a rare occasion when she actually won a discussion with Coco. Whenever she thought she was losing, her mother would just make something up and run with it.

After dinner, Hannah logged onto her laptop and spent hours looking for missing dog posts. She checked everywhere she could think of – Facebook, Twitter, forums, the local council message board, she even Googled it. Her final resort was searching through Instagram for any dogs that might look similar.

It was a fruitless search. Basil didn't appear to be anywhere. Perhaps she was wrong, maybe the dog was just sad because he was in the shelter. Perhaps it had nothing to do with missing his family.

The idea didn't sit right with her, but she couldn't think of what else to do. If he had anything on him to tell her more about where he had come from, it would have been easier. She doubted Basil was his real name, despite what Harry said. If only he had worn a collar with a tag on it, anything with a clue.

Closing her laptop shut, Hannah threw herself on the bed. Staring up at the ceiling, her mind drifted from Basil to Harry. He had been really nice to her, he seemed like a genuine guy. Plus, he had waved when he could have just ignored her. It was sweet.

But it was also ridiculous to be thinking of him. It would do as much good as searching for Basil's owners – a whole big load of nothing. He probably had a girlfriend anyway. A guy that nice and good looking wouldn't be single. She was probably gorgeous with long blonde hair in a perky ponytail and a giggly voice. The complete opposite of her short, boring brown hair and sensible voice. She didn't stand a chance.

Chapter 4

The next day at the shelter, Hannah was determined to not let Basil or Harry get to her. She was there to look after all the other dogs too, she resolved to focus on them instead.

"Here's Basil's food," Cory said as she handed her a bowl of brown sludge. It did not look appetizing. As she accepted the bowl, she couldn't help but remember her resolve and inwardly groaned at how Cory had managed to wipe it away with three words.

She went to Basil's cage and slid the food inside. "Dinner time, Basil, yum yum." The dog stared at her and then the bowl. He was equally as unimpressed as he lay down again. "Come on, you've got to eat. It might not look like much but perhaps it tastes better than it smells."

He sighed as he rested his head between his paws. She knew he wouldn't move after getting into his brooding position. She left the bowl there and closed the cage.

"Just try it, okay? You have to eat something."

"When you're done there you can walk the Dalmatian puppies," Cory said over her shoulder as she left.

Hannah grabbed the leashes and went to the puppies. There were five of them, all born a few weeks prior to a dog that had been dumped at the shelter. When the owners found out about the pregnancy, they ditched her. Hannah wanted to find and strangle them for being so irresponsible and cruel. She was a beautiful dog, so gentle and placid, it wasn't fair.

The mother may have been gentle and placid, but the puppies certainly weren't. Even with a leash on each of them, they all insisted on going in five different directions. Their innate curiosity was cute but all it did was wrap Hannah up in the leads. She lost count of how many times she untangled herself.

She took them around the grassy area, trying to keep track of who had done their business and who hadn't. They were too excited to care about going potty.

Out of the corner of her eye, Hannah saw Harry talking to Basil. Her jaw dropped open when she saw the dog actually eating his dinner. Whatever sweet nothings Harry was whispering in his big ears, it was obviously working. Annoyance crept through her as she wondered why he always seemed to have a way with the animals and she didn't.

"Come on, pups, try to walk in the same direction," she sighed as she tried to corral them back to their pen. The little spotted puppies were having no piece of it, they would much prefer to run wild on the grass.

Hannah let them play for a while longer, not wanting to see them cooped up for too long. If she could make them happy by just being outside, then she could be patient while they played.

If she had to admit it, the puppies were probably some of the cutest she had ever seen. Their big eyes were full of mischief, their tails happy to wag non-stop, and teasing each other seemed to be the best game to play. Nibbling on her hand seemed like good times too.

Eventually, she had to coerce them back into the shelter. It was much easier when they were ready for a nap, having tired themselves out. Hannah smiled as she replaced them in their pen, their mom watching on carefully. She closed the door and left them to their sleep time.

Harry was the only other volunteer in the dog's room. She approached him carefully as he swept.

"So what's your trick to getting Basil to eat?" She asked, wondering if he would divulge it.

"There's no trick, you just have to be patient."

"I don't believe you."

His eyes were sparkling with mischief as he replied. "I might have sprinkled in some real chicken."

It was becoming clear to Hannah that the way to excel at the shelter was easy – you cheated. "I'll remember that for next time then." She laughed, not believing she had been thinking he was some kind of dog whisperer or something. He was just smart.

"You pick up a few secrets after a while." Harry tapped her on the arm as if trying to comfort her. Her skin burned long after he took his hand back.

She picked up the mop and started cleaning where

he had already swept. "How long have you been volunteering here?"

"Two years. I like the animals, I don't like to think of them being lonely in here," he shrugged, as if it wasn't a big deal. Two years was a long time, especially for a teenager, Hannah was impressed. Most guys couldn't commit to something for one lunch break.

"Well, you're obviously good at it, the animals are lucky to have you. Which school do you go to?"

"Arthur Heights. I haven't seen you around so I assume you go somewhere else?"

"Mapleton Central."

Hannah knew of Arthur Heights, it was a prestigious school on the edge of town. It was practically a world away from the public school she attended. It explained why she had never seen Harry before, but she couldn't help feel disappointed in the knowledge. The boys from Arthur Heights never mingled with the students of Mapleton Central unless they were on a sports field and they were wiping the floor with them – which they regularly did.

"I hope I haven't offended you," Harry said, noticing Hannah's sudden withdrawal. "It's just a school. I know we have some rivalries but it's just a good natured thing."

"No, I know," Hannah stuttered, feeling horrible for thinking he might actually have liked her. She had been so stupid, why didn't she see that coming? "Why don't you volunteer in your own neighborhood? Or don't people need shelters there?"

Harry chuckled. "We have shelters closer to home. But they all have good funding, unlike here. I thought this place could use the help more."

It was actually kind of sweet that he had even thought about it, Hannah thought to herself. The fact he had actually considered those less well off than him showed a lot of character.

She kept mopping, not wanting to say anything that would only sound embarrassing if she said it out loud. She sneaked looks at Harry as he swept. He may go to a posh school, but he was so handsome it almost hurt her eyes to watch him. There was no way he was single.

They worked in unison until the floors were sparkling clean and all the dogs had fresh water. Hannah stood at the sink, tidying up before her shift was over.

Harry approached, replacing the last of the empty bowls. He hesitated, silently debating in his mind. Before he could change his decision again, he blurted out what was causing such debate. "I'd like you to come to a party… with me. It's this weekend, I don't know if you are busy or would be interested, but I'm asking anyway. You don't know unless you ask, right? Say something, please."

Hannah stood, stunned. She wasn't sure if she had processed half of what he said. Something about a party? He was inviting her to a party? Her? Party? Her mind was frazzled trying to think of an appropriate response.

"It's okay, you don't have to say anything," Harry replied to the silence. He busied himself with the nearby rags, refolding them perfectly.

"No, it's just a lot to take in. A party, sure. I can party, I can get down and boogie." She wanted to slap herself, did she really just say that? To him? What a dork.

Yet Harry didn't seem to notice. "Really? That's great. I'll text you the details."

He didn't even look at her before hurrying away on a made-up errand. She watched him leave as the smile slowly spread across her face.

It was quickly removed as she heard her name being called. "Hannah! Hannah! I'm here to pick you up," Coco yelled out from the front counter. She couldn't have just asked for her instead? Hannah remembered to breathe and quickly walked towards the noise to shut it up.

Chapter 5

"I don't think I should go," Hannah sighed as she collapsed onto the bed. "I shouldn't have said yes, I don't know what I was thinking."

"You were thinking you were normal," Coco butted in, standing at the bedroom door. "Girls your age should be going to parties."

Hannah looked to Veronica for some support. Her best friend just shrugged. "I agree with her."

"I hate it when you two gang up on me."

"Someone's got to make sure you have a good time," Coco said, throwing her hands up into the air and disappearing down the hallway.

Veronica flicked through the clothes in her wardrobe, scrunching up her face at the considerable lack of anything she deemed party-worthy. All of Hannah's clothes were just so... boring.

"Don't you have anything sparkly?"

Hannah crawled off the bed to join her. "I don't do

sparkly. How about this outfit?" She held up a beige shift dress that was half nurse and half prison warden.

"Are you kidding?" The look on Veronica's face told her it was a clear no.

She looked at her friend, already dressed in a sequined blue skirt that was shorter than anything she owned, and a black singlet top that showed her bra. If that was what girls wore to parties, then she was stuffed.

"I shouldn't go."

"You're going and we're going to be unfashionably late if you don't hurry. Put something on and I'll wait for you downstairs." She stood with her hands on her hips as she turned to face Hannah. "And don't think of doing anything stupid like locking yourself in the bathroom. You *are* going to this party and you *will* have fun."

Hannah watched, speechless and resigned, as Veronica left her alone. She grabbed a pair of denim shorts her mother had brought and she had never worn because of their bedazzled rhinestones and a plain white top. Looking in the mirror, she didn't approve but it would have to do.

Ignoring Coco and Veronica's stares as she hurried downstairs, she went directly for the car and didn't look back. They followed shortly afterwards.

The party was held in a house four blocks from the animal shelter. Neither Hannah nor Veronica knew the host, or most of the people there for that matter. Still, they entered bravely and tried to get into the swing of things.

After ten minutes of listening to the loud music and being bumped by at least a dozen elbows, Hannah leaned in closer to her friend, having to yell to be heard. "I don't like it here, I want to go home."

"Not yet, just try to have fun. Isn't that your boy toy over there?"

Hannah followed her gaze. Sure enough, through the mass of bodies, Harry was standing by the door to the kitchen. He appeared to be looking for someone as his eyes scanned the crowd. They finally settled on Hannah, causing his face to crease into a smile. He started approaching.

"He's coming over," Hannah said, panicking now. She didn't want him to see her but she also did at the same time. It would have been far easier to stay at home watching documentaries. There was a good one about dinosaurs on.

She couldn't think of a way to disappear before Harry arrived. The first thing she noticed was how he had gone to an effort to look good. His usual messy hair was brushed, his clothes weren't wrinkled, and that beautiful smile was lighting up his entire face.

"Hey Hannah, glad you could make it." His gaze was too intense for her to think straight.

"Yeah, me too," she stuttered out. Her cheeks burned, she thought for sure she was making a fool of herself. She had never felt so self-conscious of everything.

"Would you like to dance?"

An alarm started sounding in her head. She didn't dance, she wouldn't even know how. She would only make a fool of herself, why hadn't she expected this and planned something accordingly? Where was the nearest exit?

"Sure she would," Veronica replied for her, pushing

Hannah into his arms. She couldn't stop herself before she felt his hand grip around her and lead her away. Hannah tried to make her friend burst into flames just by looking at her. If looks could kill, it would have worked.

"I don't really know how to dance," Hannah managed to get out as she stared at Harry. The light danced in his eyes, he was finding her pain funny – great.

"Just relax and move your feet. I don't really know what I'm doing either, but it doesn't matter as long as you're having fun. Right?" He placed his hands on her waist and guided her to the left and then the right. She had to move her feet to stop herself toppling over.

Before she knew it, Hannah was dancing. Well, a dorky type of dancing, but everyone else was too wrapped up in themselves to notice. Harry was the only one she cared about and he couldn't take his eyes off her.

"I'm dancing," she said, finally letting herself smile with the triumph.

"You're good, see?" He let go of her waist, letting her free to move on her own accord. Hannah was almost dizzy with the smell of his cologne, he smelt so good she wanted to get closer just so she could inhale him.

Feeling more confident, Hannah tried a few more moves than just shuffling back and forth. She wiggled around in a circle, laughing at her own terrible attempt. As she returned, she smacked Harry right across the chest.

"I'm so sorry," she hastily apologized, mortally embarrassed at her own clumsiness.

"Don't worry about it," he chuckled. "You're getting better."

She seriously doubted that but it didn't seem to matter much anymore. It was like the rest of the party had completely disappeared, leaving just the two of them on the dance floor. To make it better, she didn't feel like her usual nerdy self, she felt like the kind of girl she had only *watched* dance with a guy before. Now she was *that* girl.

Hannah closed her eyes, letting the feeling of Harry being so close sink in along with the music.

Suddenly, someone bumped into her and she felt a cold liquid spread over her top. Her white top.

"Hey, watch where you're going," Harry warned the guy. Hannah's eyes burst open, just in time to see the boy walk away – leaving his entire drink on her chest. She could feel it dripping down her bra, her stomach, and her shorts. She was completely covered in the liquid.

"I'm sorry, Hannah, he wasn't watching where he was going," Harry apologized, even though it wasn't his fault. "I'm sure there's a bathroom around here, you can dry off. It will be okay."

"No, I need to go," Hannah said resolutely. She hurried away from him before he could stop her. She weaved her way through the crowd of bodies, making it impossible for Harry to follow her. She heard her name being called out several times but didn't stop or look back.

Along the way, she grabbed Veronica by the arm and continued to drag her towards the door. They were leaving, whether she liked it or not.

Outside, the air was warm and balmy. Hannah

called her mom and told her to get there as quickly as possible. She had no intentions of sticking around.

"What happened to you?" Veronica said once she had hung up, staring at the wet patch that was making her shirt see-through.

"Some idiot spilt his drink on me, what does it look like happened?"

"We don't have to leave, you can just dry off. In this weather, it won't take long."

"I don't want to dry off, I want to go home. We should never have come in the first place." She stomped off to the road, desperately wishing to see her mother's car. "I don't belong in a place like this, I think the universe was making that point obvious."

Veronica laughed, only making her grumpier. "It wasn't the universe that spilled their drink on you, it was some idiot. You're such a drama queen."

"I'm not a drama queen, I'm realistic."

Finally, the car appeared. It had barely come to a halt before Hannah was inside and slamming the door behind her. Veronica did the same on the other side.

"Drive, Mom, please," Hannah directed, waiting for the comments that would surely come from her mother.

She stepped on the accelerator before opening her mouth. "I thought you girls would stay at the party longer. Was it boring?" She grimaced as if being bored was the worst thing on the planet.

Veronica replied before Hannah could. "Someone spilt their drink on Hannah and she saw it as a sign from above that she needed to leave."

"Oh, honey, I'm sorry," Coco cooed, even though she wasn't taking the situation seriously. Did she not see how wet and transparent her shirt was? "Maybe next time you'll have more fun."

"She was having fun before that," Veronica volunteered. "She was dancing with the guy she's crushing on."

"You were dancing?"

Hannah was doing her best to ignore them but it wasn't working. Everything they said just twisted the knife in her chest. "Yes, I was dancing, call the newspapers. I'm not the freak you both think I am."

"This guy, is he cute?" Coco asked, ignoring the outburst.

"He's gorgeous," Veronica answered, knowing Hannah wouldn't. "And he's totally into her."

"He won't be now," Hannah mumbled, wondering if she could get anything right. Anything at all would have been nice.

Chapter 6

"I'm not getting out of bed, I'm going to stay here forever and be a crazy cat lady for the rest of my life," Hannah insisted as Coco tried to pull the covers off her. She had no intention of getting out of bed and facing the world, not after the embarrassment of the previous night. No way.

"Crazy cat ladies can't give me grandchildren one day. You are getting up," Coco said through gritted teeth, holding onto the bedcovers. They had a tug of war, not only with the sheets but with their will too.

Within the hour, Coco was dropping Hannah off at the shelter, barely stopping to let her out. She skidded off into the distance with a screech, there was no going back now.

Cory directed her to the office where her task of the day was going to be paperwork filing. It wasn't the most exciting of jobs but it did mean Hannah could avoid seeing Harry – if he was working that morning.

If was far easier to avoid him altogether than have to speak with him. Not after she had run out of the party with a see-through shirt.

Even in the office, the sound of the dogs barking, the cats meowing, and a goat bleating could be heard through the walls. Hannah briefly wondered how noisy it must have been on Noah's ark. Probably a lot worse than in the shelter – and there would be no way to get away from it.

Flicking through the paperwork and trying to put it into alphabetical order, one of the records caught her eye. It was Basil's report from when he first arrived at the shelter. She pulled it out and read through.

Basil was reportedly found wandering the streets in Mapleton, across town from the shelter. The girl who dropped her off said she didn't see anyone who owned him and didn't want to leave him there so she immediately drove to the shelter.

The report was brief and to the point. The veterinarian on duty had given him an exam, Basil had passed with flying colors. He was thin, but it wasn't anything to worry about unless he continued to lose weight. He was assigned a number and a cage, and he had been there ever since.

Hannah found a notepad and wrote down the woman's name and address. She wasn't sure what she would do with it, but she had to find out more about Basil. Perhaps the woman was the only clue she was ever going to get. She pocketed the sheet of paper.

"Hey, here you are." Harry's voice filled the room, scaring her half to death. She jumped, sending the paperwork scattering to the floor.

She ignored the papers for a moment and turned to

face him instead, what was another embarrassment?

He was holding Basil, absentmindedly petting his head. "Cory has you doing paperwork?"

"Yeah, someone's got to do it." She tried to think cool thoughts, desperately trying to keep the blushing from her cheeks. She wished she had the sole superpower of controlling it.

"Look, I was trying to find you because I wanted to see how you were," Harry started. "I'm sorry last night didn't go exactly as planned."

And there it was, the memory that was sure to inflame her cheeks. It was the last thing Hannah wanted to talk about. She changed the subject instead, completely ignoring him.

"I want to find Basil's owners," she blurted out from desperation. "I have the details of the woman who found him. I want to speak with her."

"Great, we'll go after our shift."

It wasn't what she had intended. She said it to get away from him, not spend more time making a fool of herself in his company.

"You don't have to come with me," she replied, trying not to look him in the eyes. They were her kryptonite.

"I want to." He smiled, she made the mistake of noticing. Perhaps it wouldn't be so bad, maybe they could just forget about the night before? Miracles happened all the time, right?

"Alrighty then."

Harry left her to the paperwork while she breathed a sigh of relief. She didn't leave the office for the rest of her shift, refusing to put herself at risk of further embarrassment.

A part of her hoped Harry would completely forget about visiting the woman. But at one o'clock exactly, his face appeared at the doorway, still locked in a grin.

"Are you ready?" He asked, leaving no room for her to back out.

Hannah nodded and they signed out of the shelter. Their modes of transport were bicycles, parked at the side of the building. They put on their helmets and started in the direction of the woman's house.

Once Hannah relaxed a little, she found herself actually having fun with Harry. They weaved through the roads, letting the wind run through her hair. It was a cooling breeze on the otherwise hot summer day.

Harry didn't race ahead, even though she knew he was capable of going must faster than her. Instead, he made sure to stay by her side, setting a steady pace the entire way. Whenever she looked over at him, he was doing the same to her. It made her giggle every time.

They finally reached the address – 221 Roseland Way – and knocked on the front door. Hannah prayed someone would be home and willing to talk to two kids about a dog she found three months ago.

Just when they thought nobody would answer, a woman opened the door. She eyed the pair suspiciously, hoping they weren't selling anything.

"Hello, are you Wendy Wong?" Hannah asked, trying to be as polite as possible.

"Yes, and you are?" She stood with her arms crossed, obviously not trying to be polite to the strangers.

"My name is Hannah and this is Harry, we work at the Mapleton Animal Rescue Centre. You dropped off a dog three months ago?"

Wendy nodded. "I did."

Harry picked up the conversation. "We were hoping you might be able to tell us some more details about where you found him?"

"We're trying to find his owners," Hannah added.

She hesitated before continuing. "I found him in Rochedale Street, he was just wandering about by himself. He was awfully thin and it didn't look like anyone looked after him. So I dropped him at the shelter and they took it from there. I don't have much else to say, really."

"Rochedale Street?" Hannah asked, trying to place the street. It was across town like the report had said but it wasn't a nice neighborhood. Basil didn't seem like the kind of dog you'd keep for guard duty.

"Yeah, that's the street," Wendy replied. "I've got stuff to do, are there any more questions?"

Harry exchanged a glance with Hannah, they obviously weren't going to get any magical information out of the woman. "That's all, thank you for your time."

Without saying goodbye, Wendy closed the door on them. They retreated back to their bikes, a little forlorn about not getting anywhere.

"I think we need ice cream," Harry declared. "You up for it?"

Not believing she was about to agree, Hannah said: "Sure."

She followed him to the nearest corner store where he emerged with two ice cream cones full of chocolate goodness. She accepted one and they sat on the sidewalk to eat them.

The silence was painful. Hannah knew what she

wanted to say but wasn't sure if she was brave enough to do it. Or that she could get through it without sounding like an idiot. She decided to stay on a safe topic instead – for now.

"I think we should walk around Rochedale Street and see if anyone knows Basil."

"I think that's our best shot at finding his owner," Harry agreed. "We will need to take some photos of him to show people."

"Maybe we could make posters too so we can put them up around the place."

His grin returned. "Yeah, it will be fun."

The blanket of silence threatened them again. This time, Hannah was ready. "I'm sorry about running out on you last night. I had a really good time up until then."

"I did too. I thought I might have said or done something wrong which is why you didn't come back." His grin was gone, instead he was staring intently at his ice cream.

She hadn't thought he would react like that. Blaming himself? That was ridiculous, did he not realize she was out of his league? He could have had any girl at the party, she never in a million years thought he would give her another thought once she left. In her head, he had just found another girl to dance with and partied hard for the rest of the night.

"You didn't do anything, you were perfect in fact."

His head shot up, their eyes locked. "So why'd you leave?"

"I was embarrassed. And my shirt was see-through." The reasons now seemed so stupid. She started laughing. "I guess I panicked."

He placed his hand on her arm, the warmth of it burned on her skin in a wonderfully tingly way. "Next time you panic, let me know and I'll talk you out of it. Deal?"

"Deal."

She covered his hand with hers, wondering if this was how good things began.

Chapter 7

The wait for work the next day was practically impossible. Coco didn't need to get Hannah out of bed, she was waiting by the front door to say goodbye.

Cycling like an Olympian, Hannah was inside the shelter with her camera before her shift was due to start. She waited for Harry, he practically followed her in.

She held up her camera. "Do you think Basil's ready for his close up?"

"One way to find out," he grinned in return. They took the depressed dog from his cage and placed him on the grass outside. The sun was shining on them all from a cloudless blue sky. They couldn't have asked for better weather.

Hannah brushed Basil's fur, trying to get it to stay down. The unruly follicles wouldn't do as they should. "I guess his owner will recognize the bad hair day," she shrugged, giving up. Just like the dog himself, his

36

hair refused to do as it was told.

"Smile, Basil," Harry commanded. He held up a treat, hoping it would inspire the dog to follow directions. He should have known better.

"He's a typical model, huh?" Hannah giggled. "He won't eat, he won't do as he's told, and he looks sad."

"I'm surprised he got out of bed for less than ten thousand dollars."

Despite the unwilling model, together they managed to snap enough decent photos of Basil to make posters. Harry carried him back inside after he refused to walk anymore.

"We're going to find your family," Hannah whispered, promising the dog. She was determined to come through for him, no matter what it took.

They attended to the other dogs and cats before having some time to use the computer in the small office. Checking with Cory, she was happy for them to print up posters for Basil.

Hannah sat in front of the computer and started typing, uploading Basil's photo and making sure it stood out on the page.

She held up the finished product. "What do you think?"

Harry took it, making sure to examine it carefully. The phone number was correct, the picture was clear, and the message was in a big font. "It's perfect."

Hannah beamed with pride. They finished their shift and rode over to Rochedale Street – the scene of the crime. They started at the end of the street and went knocking on each door. Hannah took the left side of the street and Harry took the right. They met up at the end.

"Did you have any luck?" Harry asked, hoping for a positive answer.

He would have to wait a while longer. "Nobody recognizes him. It's like Basil just fell from the sky. We're never going to find his family, I'm going to let him down."

Harry shook his head, refusing to believe it. "We just need to keep going. I know we can do this. Come on, there's plenty more streets around here."

He held out his hand, unwilling to take it back until she placed hers in his. She eventually did, letting herself be led down the next street.

They canvassed the houses until the sun threatened to dip below the horizon. On every light pole, they taped a poster of Basil, hoping someone would recognize him and get in touch. They were fast running out of ideas.

Harry cycled with Hannah back to her place, refusing to let her go alone in the dark. It meant it would take him twice as long to get home but he insisted anyway. The thought brought a smile to her face and her heart swelled with happiness.

"I'll see you tomorrow," Harry said, ready to depart.

"Thanks for… everything today."

"You're worth it. I mean, you're welcome," he quickly corrected himself.

She couldn't be sure, but through the dim light Hannah thought she could see a rosy blush to his cheeks at his fumble. It only made him even more adorable.

"Get home safely."

Harry nodded, saluted, and started peddling down

the street. She stood on the front stoop, watching him until he was out of sight. She seriously wondered if she would ever be able to get the smile off her lips. Even if they hadn't got their big breakthrough, she still had a wonderful day. And he was the sole reason for it.

She tried to hide her happiness as she entered the house, trying to avoid the twenty questions from Coco. Hannah wouldn't have been surprised to find her watching them through the window, but thankfully she was in the living room – well away from the front door.

As she stepped into the room, she was surprised to see Veronica waiting for her. "Hey, what are you doing here?"

"I've got news," Veronica replied excitedly.

"Come upstairs then." Hannah looked pointedly at her mother, the one woman who didn't know the meaning of the word *boundaries*.

They retreated to the privacy of Hannah's bedroom and closed the door. "So, what's this big news?"

Veronica bit her bottom lip, trying to draw out the excitement she felt. "Lucas asked me out. We're going to the movies on Friday night!"

"Wow, that is news. When did this happen?" Hannah sat on the edge of her bed, completely absorbed in the story now.

"About half an hour ago. He called me out of nowhere, I don't even know how he got my phone number."

Veronica had a crush on Lucas since Hannah could remember. He was always the one they had to spy on at school and linger around at dances. Hannah had suspected he was a lost cause but she was happy to be proven wrong.

"How are you going to survive until Friday night?" Hannah laughed. "It's three whole days away."

"I know, right?" She clutched at her heart, as if it might just burst out suddenly. "When we're a couple, we could double date with you and Harry."

Hannah liked the sound of that – double date. But then again, they hadn't really even been on a single date yet. "We might have to wait until Harry and I are a couple first."

"It's not official? I thought you really liked him."

"I do, I'm just not sure if he's so into it yet."

Veronica waved her words away. "I've seen the way he looks at you, and trust me, he's into you."

"The way he looks at me?" Hannah had no idea what she was talking about. He only looked at her like every other person on the planet.

"Oh please, you haven't noticed?" Veronica watched her shrug, rolling her eyes before she continued. "It's like he's a starving zombie and you've got the yummiest brains around. It won't be long before he wants a taste."

"I'm not sure-" She was interrupted by her mother as she burst through the door – without knocking.

"She means he wants to kiss you," Coco said, matter-of-factly. "Is this the boy you went to the party for?"

"Mom, get out," Hannah groaned. It was bad enough dealing with boys and the unfamiliar territory, let alone trying to explain it all to her mother too.

"I have a right to know who is trying to get their hands on my little baby. I want to meet this boy."

Hannah stood and started pushing Coco towards

the door, refusing to listen. "I'll introduce you when you aren't so crazy. If it even goes anywhere with him."

"Oh, it will," Coco said before having the door closed on her face. Hannah pressed her ear to the door, listening for the footsteps before believing she had gone.

Veronica gave her a look, the one she always did when Coco interfered, it said *I understand*. For the first time, Hannah couldn't let her mother bring her down, she was too happy.

"I hope crazy isn't hereditary," she giggled. "Now, tell me everything about what Lucas said."

Veronica did just that, it took almost an hour to describe the one minute phone call. Hannah listened intently, only interrupting when a question was needed for more information. They spent the rest of the night talking and laughing.

By the time morning came around, Hannah was running late for the shelter. She peddled her bicycle as fast as she could, trying to make up for lost time.

Harry was already there, cleaning out the cat's litter trays. She took over holding the bag for him.

"How's Basil doing today?" She asked, hoping he might have snapped out of his depression.

"Much the same, he didn't eat the snack I gave him," Harry replied sadly. "Hopefully someone will see our posters."

"I hope so," Hannah agreed. They made their way through each of the cages and then moved onto the dogs. It was time for their daily activities.

Unlocking the doors, Hannah watched as the dogs eagerly took off towards the sunshine. Their happiness was unbridled as their tails wagged all over the place.

"I hope they all get homes soon," Hannah commented as a little brown puppy licked at her hand. "They deserve to be with a family that loves them."

Harry laughed as he was simultaneously attacked by a legion of over-excited animals. They pushed him backwards until he was lying on the ground. From there, they could really start their licking and nipping campaign.

"I think they'll do fine," he said, trying to regain his breath. "They'll all stay here until they're adopted and they've got us for the rest of the summer."

Hannah liked that word: *us.* He was no longer talking singular, but including her in his plans for the rest of the holidays. She couldn't help but smile at the thought.

She started running around the grassed area, getting the dogs to chase her and use up their energy. She giggled the entire time as she tried to avoid getting captured. They all ran after her with such glee on their faces. It would be a crime if they weren't all adopted soon.

"Harry, phone," Cory called out from the door. She laughed at seeing the chaos that was ensuing. "Some woman says she saw your poster."

Hannah and Harry exchanged a glance before he ran for the phone.

Chapter 8

Hannah paced, trying not to get her hopes up. She absentmindedly played with the dogs, wishing she could hear what Harry was saying through the window. He kept nodding, was that a good or bad sign? She didn't know, it was making her nauseous.

Just because someone had seen their poster, it didn't mean they knew who Basil was. Or who his family was either, for that matter. It just meant they had seen the poster. Heaps of people probably saw the posters, they had plastered them on every available space they could.

She knew the odds of finding Basil's family were slim to none. He had been there for three months, probably long forgotten as having run away or perished. She shouldn't get her hopes up.

The call seemed to last an interminable amount of time. Each second that passed by was like a dagger in her side, only serving to make her even more anxious.

She wished and hoped and prayed it was the news they all wanted to hear.

Finally, Harry hung up and stepped back outside into the play area. Hannah stood, planted in place by her anxiety, and ignoring the puppies tugging at her skirt. She feared and needed the information he had. "Well?"

Harry stopped directly in front of her, his face betraying nothing of the news. "That call was about Basil."

"I know, what did they say?"

The moments passed by, each one making her heart wrench tighter. She thought she just might have a heart attack.

Harry's face twisted into an impossibly wide smile. "They said Basil belongs to them."

"It was his family?" She didn't believe she had heard right, it couldn't be the news they were hoping for. Could it?

He nodded. In the elation of the news and without thinking, he swept Hannah into his arms and planted his lips on hers. Shock registered in her brain at the kiss before she let it go. His lips were so soft on hers, but so perfect too. She had never been kissed before and this was a wonderful first attempt.

She didn't want to let go, she wanted to stay there in that moment forever – capture it like a photograph so she could remember it over and over again. The heat of his body so close was making her blush, but she didn't want him to move away – not even an inch.

Finally, he let her go and wrapped his arms around to hug her instead. They stood there, amongst a dozen excited dogs, for longer than was polite.

When he eventually took his arms back, Hannah's head was giddy with the whole thing. She didn't know what she was supposed to say or do.

Using her tried and trusted method, she decided to ignore what just happened. She could analyze it later with Veronica. "Are they coming to get Basil?"

"They're coming in this afternoon to pick him up."

"We should get him ready then." She waited until Harry nodded in agreement before herding the dogs back inside. They would get another run later on, right now they had a dog with a very important meeting.

Standing in front of Basil's cage, they both looked at him like proud parents with a secret. Harry spoke first. "Basil, you're going home."

The dog looked unconvinced, he barely raised an eyelid to look at him. Undeterred, they took him from his cage and put him straight into the bathtub. He stood in the water like he was pretending he was elsewhere while they scrubbed, shampooed, and brushed him until he was dry again.

Completing the makeover, Hannah placed a red bow around his neck, determined he would look his best for the reunion.

"How's he look?" She asked proudly. At the very least, he smelt a lot better than he did before. Now he smelt like cherries.

"Perfect," Harry declared as he gave Basil the once over. He took his head between his hands. "It's been a pleasure knowing you, boy. I hope you live a long and happy life with your family."

"And don't get out again," Hannah added. "We don't want to see you back here again. But I mean that in the nicest possible way."

"He knows." Harry grinned and released his head again.

As she hugged Basil for the last time, she was overcome with sadness. "I'm kind of sad to see him go." She had spent countless hours trying to cheer him up, spending time with him so he would know he wasn't alone in the world.

"I know, you get attached to them when they're here for so long."

She gave Basil a kiss and let him go, just as the bell rang from the front reception area. She looked at Harry and took a deep breath. "I guess this is it."

"Hopefully."

Cory appeared through the doorway. "Basil's family is here."

With one last pat, they guided Basil through to the front reception area of the shelter. He walked like he always did, with his head down and slowly. Even after his makeover he was still depressed.

Standing in the room wasn't just the woman Harry spoke with on the telephone, but her husband and three children too. The five of them stood there anxiously awaiting, hoping Basil was indeed their missing family member.

The moment the door was opened, Basil sprung to life. He lifted his head and ran for the family, his tail wagging so fast it was at risk of falling off.

"Charlie!" They all called out in unison as the dog reached them. He was instantly enthralled in a round of hugs and kisses.

Hannah could feel tears welling in her eyes. She tried to blink them away but it was impossible. Basil was a completely different dog, he was happy for the first time since she had met him. He had found his family, he was whole again. She knew he wasn't just a moping dog, she knew he was missing people and now he was reunited with them. It was too much not to cry.

She looked over just as Harry wiped at his own eyes. He tried to cover it, but she still saw. She slipped her hand into his, offering him some silent comfort.

"Thank you so much for finding Charlie," the woman said, her eyes filled with tears too. "I really can't thank you enough. We never thought we'd see him again."

"How did he get away?" Cory asked, all business. She had seen too many reunions to be affected anymore.

"We went away for the weekend and left someone to housesit," the woman explained while her kids were all over the dog. "They accidently left the door open and he took off. We looked everywhere for him but it was like he just vanished. We thought perhaps he was stolen. Where did you find him?"

"He was found in Rochedale Street and brought here three months ago."

"That's at least ten miles from our house. I can't believe it's been so long. We thought for sure something bad had happened to him. When I saw the poster, I didn't want to get my hopes up and believe it could be him but I knew in my heart it was."

"He's certainly happy to see you," Hannah commented. "He really missed you all."

"I'd like to make a donation to your shelter," the man said as he pulled out his check book. "We want to make sure you have the funds to look after many other dogs just like Charlie."

"Donations are always accepted," Cory smiled.

They said their final goodbyes before the family left. As they stepped out the door, Basil turned and gave them one last look – they could swear it was a smile. He wagged his tail and followed his family to the car.

Harry led Hannah back into the shelter, never letting go of her hand. It was his now, there was no way he was going to give it back.

She sighed. "I'm so glad I came through on my promise to Basil. Or, uh, Charlie."

"I still think he looked like a Basil," Harry joked, trying to lighten the mood. "But I guess Charlie was a good name too."

"I guess we'd better get back to work. We've got a lot more to do."

"What do you mean? We've done all our chores here for the day." Harry looked around, trying to see what she saw.

Hannah grinned. "There are still a lot of homeless animals here. Which one are we going to find a home for next?"

He returned her smile, finally seeing it, the long row of cages. They *did* have a lot more work to do. But they had all summer, and each other. They could do it.

ꙮ The End ꙮ

A Hairy Tail 2

Dedication

For Tom.

Chapter 1

There were so many kittens surrounding Hannah she thought for sure they were going to overpower her. But they were so delicate and fluffy that they wouldn't be able to do anything except kill her with cuteness. It wouldn't be a bad way to go.

She giggled to herself as she stopped two of the little cats from being tangled in her shoelaces. All the kittens were less than a month old, they weighed practically nothing and were still trying to get used to walking. They were adorable in their clumsiness.

Hannah stood in the middle of them, unable to even comprehend being able to find homes for them all. They couldn't stay at the animal shelter forever; they needed to be placed into homes so they could be part of a family. That was her mission, but she had no idea how she was going to do it.

She suddenly felt arms snake around her waist, locking together over her stomach. She leaned back into Harry, feeling right at home in his arms.

"I don't know what's cuter, you or these kittens," he whispered in her ear, just loud enough for only the two of them to hear.

Hannah couldn't stop the smile spreading across her face, nor could she remove it. Ever since she met Harry, she didn't think she would ever be able to erase that smile. There was something about him that had such an effect on her, like she was struck with lightning every time he was near.

"You're such a liar," she teased back at him, holding onto his arms so he couldn't take them away. "But I like you anyway."

"I'm not lying, it's a difficult decision."

"I would vote for the kittens, nothing beats a kitten for cuteness."

He leant his head on her shoulder in defeat, giving up. "Fine. But you are a very close runner up."

He dropped his arms to crouch down and pick up two of the grey kittens. They pawed at him playfully, tiny in his hands. The mother watched on from the side, too tired to do anything about it. She was over her protectiveness, there were too many to mollycoddle.

Hannah sat on the ground and stroked the mom; she had done well looking after her babies. She deserved a rest. "How are we going to find them all homes?"

Harry shrugged. "I don't know. We might have to put up a serious amount of posters to let people know we have more kittens than we know what to do with."

"We could convince the radio to make an announcement. Or set up an information booth somewhere. We could fundraise at the same time." Hannah was instantly excited by the idea. Spending her summer volunteering at the animal shelter was one thing, but she didn't want to stop there. Not after all the good she had seen take place within the walls.

"All excellent ideas," Cory commented from the door. "Feel free to do it, we need all the help we can get. It's been a bumper kitten season this year."

"I can't believe people can just dump their cats like this," Hannah muttered, picking up a little tabby. "Who wouldn't want these little guys?"

"Plenty of people, trust me," Cory said before she retreated back into her office. She was the manager of the shelter, there nearly twenty-four hours a day to make sure everything ran smoothly.

The bell on the reception door rang, signaling an end to their kitten time. Hannah and Harry carefully placed their cats back onto the ground and hurried through to the public area, hoping it wasn't another delivery of unwanted babies.

A woman stood there, not holding any animals but with her brow wrinkled in distress.

"Can I help you?" Hannah asked, fearing there must be something seriously wrong with their visitor. She was clearly in distress.

"My dog is missing, I can't find her anywhere. Please, you have to help me find her." The words came so fast they both had to concentrate to understand her.

Harry pulled out a missing animal report sheet. "We will need to fill in this report and then we can see if she's here anywhere. What type of dog is it?"

"A Cocker Spaniel. Her name's Lolly and she's only

a puppy. She can't look after herself, she won't last a night out in the cold."

Hannah wanted to point out that it was summer and the nights were still balmy, there was no chance of the dog freezing to death, but she held her tongue. The poor woman was in enough distress.

"We haven't had any Cocker Spaniels come into the shelter," Harry replied. "But we can keep a lookout for Lolly and call you if someone turns her in."

"I guess that's something," the woman sighed.

Harry ran through the rest of the form with her, covering everything from when she last saw Lolly to how she might have escaped. According to the woman, the dog was locked in her yard with absolutely no way of escaping – by herself anyway. She mentioned Lolly was being trained to compete in dog shows. If she didn't get her back, then she would have to start all over again with a new dog. And she would probably be too heartbroken to do that.

"We'll call you if Lolly comes in," Hannah said, giving her a comforting smile. She didn't have any pets herself but could imagine how awful it would be to have one missing. It wasn't like they could call and let you know they were safe. It was unlikely the puppy would even be able to find her way home if she got lost.

"Please look out for her, I can't live without my little Lolly," the woman begged before casting one more heart wrenching look their way. She shuffled out, leaving them both feeling awful for her loss.

"You're getting good at filling in those reports," Hannah pointed out once they were alone again. "How many is that this week?"

"That's the fifth one in less than a week."

"That's a lot of dogs to go missing, is that normal?"

Harry shook his head sadly. "I've never heard of that many being missing before."

"A run of people being careless?" Hannah offered. It was summer and people did tend to be outdoors more. That could easily lead to more gates being accidently left open, more dogs escaping their leash in the parks, any number of things.

"Probably," Harry agreed before taking a step closer to her. "I hope you remember our date tonight? Prepare to have your mind blown."

"You talk it up enough, I hope you can live up to my expectation," Hannah teased. Harry had been talking about their first official date for days. He wouldn't reveal any of the details, just teased her with hints. So far, she knew it had something to do with water and there would be dinner involved. She was clueless about what he had arranged.

"I offer a money back guarantee if you're not completely satisfied." Hannah blushed as he took her hand. "Trust me, it will be spectacular. I'll pick you up at eight."

She nodded and watched him disappear into the back of the shelter. Thinking about their date made her terrified and excited at the same time. Either she was going to spend the entire night freaking out, or she would be able to relax and enjoy it. It could still go either way.

She picked up the missing pet report and filed it with the others, hoping they would all get resolved soon.

Chapter 2

The minute Hannah stepped into her house, she felt like running right back out again. She had made a huge mistake telling both her mom and best friend about her big date. As she looked at both of them, grinning like fools in front of her, she vowed she wouldn't make that mistake again.

"What are you doing here?" She asked Veronica, hoping for a good explanation and not the one she was expecting from her friend.

"I've come to get you ready for your date." That was what she was afraid of.

"I'm just going to change into something comfortable and brush my hair. I don't need a duo of stylists," Hannah insisted.

"Don't be silly," Coco, her mother, said with a roll of the eyes. "You need to look your best for your little friend."

"Please don't call him my little friend. His name is

Harry, you can call him Harry."

"I call him the hottie," Veronica grinned as she took her hand and pulled her up the stairs. Coco followed closely, carrying her hairdryer in one hand and curling iron in the other. It was Hannah's worst nightmare come true.

Once in her bedroom, Veronica pushed Hannah into the seat in front of her dressing table. "You start on the hair and I'll find something for her to wear."

Coco nodded as she disappeared into Hannah's closet. "Do you want your hair up or down, Honey?"

"Just down. I only need to brush it," Hannah insisted, eying the torture devices in her hand. She had suffered at the hands of the curling iron before. She still had the burn mark on her neck to prove it.

Coco pursed her lips in thought. "I think it would look better up. You'll see."

It was pointless to argue. Hannah could only sit there as her mother pulled and prodded at her brown hair. Veronica emerged from the closet with a few outfits flung over her arm.

"Where did he say he was taking you?" She asked.

"He didn't, it's a surprise."

"That doesn't help to know what the dress code is," Veronica pouted. "Smart or casual? Did he give you any hints?"

"None that would help. I was just going to wear my jeans and a top."

Coco and Veronica exchanged a glance, one that screamed she was clueless. "You can't wear jeans to your first official date. How about this dress? It can be worn dressed up or down." Veronica held up a baby blue dress she hadn't seen in ages. Her mother had bought it for her in an attempt to get her to be more girly.

Her immediate reaction was to say no, but Hannah stopped herself. Perhaps Harry would like her in it? She always only wore shorts around the shelter; maybe it would be good to be a little bit girly. The thought surprised her as much as the others.

"I think that dress would be perfect," she said. "But I think I need to wear my hair in just a simple ponytail. Nothing fancy, Mom, I'm not going to the prom."

"You got it, Honey," Coco replied. She proceeded to follow orders, something she very rarely did. When she had tamed the hair into an elastic, they both waited for her to change.

The Hannah that emerged from the bathroom was not the Hannah they knew. The blue dress fit her perfectly, showing off her curves in all the right places. Curves neither of them knew even existed.

"Well? What do you think?" Hannah asked nervously, twirling in place so they could get the full three-sixty view.

"You look beautiful," they both gushed in unison. They insisted on taking photos before she was allowed to wait downstairs for her beau.

Hannah couldn't sit still. She paced in the hallway, waiting for the doorbell to ring. If he didn't come soon, she was going to wear herself out just with the nerves.

Finally, the bell sounded. She swung open the door, beating Coco and Veronica to it. Harry was standing on the porch, a bunch of daisy flowers clutched in his hands. He held them out. "These are for you."

She took them, her stomach sick with butterflies.

"Thank you."

"Are you ready?"

"Yep." She handed the flowers to her mother. "See you later."

"Don't be later than eleven o'clock."

"Don't be good," Veronica added.

Hannah ignored them both and left the safety of her home to step out into the unknown. They reached the end of the path. She wasn't entirely sure what she had been expecting, but it wasn't Harry's bicycle.

"Should I get my bike?" She asked, starting to wonder if the dress was such a good idea after all.

"Absolutely not," Harry replied as if appalled by the very idea. He climbed onto the seat and patted the handlebars. "You're arriving in style tonight."

Hannah laughed. "Is that really safe?"

He held out his hand expectantly, waiting for her to let him help her on. "I won't let anything hurt you. I promise to deliver you home in one piece."

She didn't need anything else to convince her. She accepted the hand and pulled herself onto the handlebars of his bike. He pulled her back, letting her rest on his chest. She had to admit, it did feel pretty safe there.

Racing through the streets, Hannah felt the wind in her hair like she was flying. The air was warm and the moon sat high in the crystal clear sky. They couldn't have got better weather if they tried.

"Where are we going?" She asked.

"So impatient. You'll see for yourself in a minute," Harry replied, still refusing to give away any details.

Hannah took the hint and kept all her questions to herself. She tried to relax and just let it all happen.

9

There was no point in stressing about the date, she was with Harry and everything would be fine.

They approached a steep track and Hannah finally got a hint about where they were headed. She gripped onto the handlebars, not wanting to go over them accidently. She knew the track headed down towards Shelly Beach.

So they were headed to the beach, but there was nothing else down there. Hadn't he mentioned eating dinner? It only helped to confuse her even more.

Harry applied the brakes and they glided down to stop at the beachfront. They climbed off the bike and he led her onto the sand. They didn't stop until they reached the harder sand nearer the water.

"This is the perfect spot," Harry declared. "Wait here for a second and I'll be right back."

Hannah watched him hurry away. Standing alone on the beach she couldn't work out what on earth he was doing. The only light was emanating from the moon so it wasn't long before she lost sight of him completely. For just a moment, she wondered if he would leave her there. Some people might find it funny, but surely not Harry. He liked her, right?

She stressed the entire time until he re-emerged with a wide grin on his face. In his hands was a basket, God only knows where he got it from.

"What's that?" Hannah asked, feeling a little guilty for doubting him.

"Dinner..." With that said, Harry proceeded to pull a blanket from the basket. He placed it on the sand with a flurry, settling it evenly. Kneeling down, he then pulled out two containers of food, cutlery, and a bottle of soda. "...is served."

He completed the arrangement with a battery operated lantern, settling it on the blanket so they could see what they were doing without having to squint. Hannah sat, amazed at the spread he had put on.

"Harry, this is amazing," she gushed without thinking. "Did you seriously go to all this effort by yourself?"

"Of course I did, I told you our first official date would be epic."

"This is epic."

"I know," he smiled, the lantern reflecting in his eyes and making them sparkle. "Now, eat."

He dished out the food – chicken and salad – before they started to eat. The only sound that filtered through to them were the crashing waves. That evening it was like nothing else existed in the world except them, the water, and the stars. It was perfectly magical, a night Hannah could never have dreamed would actually happen to her.

"That star up there," Harry said as they were finishing their meal. He pointed to the sky at a particularly bright star. "It's called the Venetian Star because it sparkles like the sun hitting glass."

"That's a lie," Hannah giggled. Her and her father used to always go star gazing when she was little. She could name each of the constellations like they were a shopping list.

"Okay, it's a lie, I have no idea. But it's still pretty, right?"

"Very much so."

"You look really pretty tonight," Harry said, still keeping his gaze skywards. "I forgot to say that when I picked you up, sorry."

"You don't need to apologize." Hannah looked everywhere else but at him too. She didn't want him to see her face red with blushing.

"I thought it, but I was too nervous to say it."

Hannah couldn't keep the smile from her face; it was possibly the sweetest thing anyone had ever said to her. "You look really nice tonight too. I thought it and didn't say it either."

"I'm really glad you're here."

"I'm glad you're here too." The butterflies were beginning to start in her stomach again. Was he going to kiss her? Would he make his move? She didn't know what he would do and the thought made her head swirl with anticipation in the best way possible. She continued to look at the stars, keeping watch on him from the corner of her eye.

Heavy panting interrupted the moment. It definitely wasn't Harry. A Labrador dog raced through them, digging at the blanket.

"Hey boy," Harry exclaimed as he patted him. "What are you doing here?"

Hannah looked around and saw his owner racing down the beach with an empty leash. "I think he's an escape artist." She pointed at the owner as he made his way across the sand. She giggled as the dog's wagging tail hit her on the leg repeatedly.

"Sorry, he got away from me," the man quickly apologized as he reached them. "Come on, Barney, back on the lead."

The dog went away happily with his owner, his tail wagging well into the distance. "He reminded me of Basil," Harry commented. "I wonder how he's doing?"

"He's probably much happier with his family than he ever was at the shelter."

"No doubt. He was the most stubborn dog I've ever met."

Hannah nodded in agreement, smiling at the memory. "That's true, but at least he was cute. I hope we can reunite more dogs with their owners, I can't help but worry about all those missing dog reports."

"I know. I can't help but think there might be more to it."

"How so?" Hannah asked, hearing the seriousness in his tone. Something was obviously bothering him about it.

"Five dogs just this week, that's a lot of dogs. What if something else is going on? Like someone's taking them or something?"

Hannah didn't even want to consider the idea. Someone taking people's pets? It was appalling. "Could someone really do that?"

"People can do anything."

"That would take an evil person to do-" She didn't get to finish her sentence as suddenly a huge wave reached them. It took no time in completely saturating them and all of the picnic gear.

Both Harry and Hannah quickly jumped up, trying to keep a hold of anything they could before it was washed out to sea. They managed to rescue most things but they were drenched with the cold water.

They exchanged a look, both of them seeing how suddenly disheveled and sodden the other was. It took them only two seconds before they burst out laughing.

"The water's in my shoes," Harry commented. "It squishes when I walk."

Hannah was going to give him no sympathy. "Try wearing a dress. My underwear is completely soaked."

"Okay, you win."

They erupted into another round of giggles. Hannah tried to catch her breath as they put everything back into the wet picnic basket. She figured she probably looked terrible considering her clothes were now sticking to her and her hair was completely ruined and stringy. At least she wasn't alone.

"I think the universe is telling us to go home," Harry said. "What do you think?"

"I think it was pretty clear," Hannah agreed. She followed him back to his bicycle, the squelching of his shoes the only sound apart from the lapping waves.

He positioned the basket on the back of the bike and climbed onto the seat. He waited, guiding Hannah onto the handlebars. They dripped a trail of water the entire way home.

When they pulled up outside Hannah's house, the butterflies in her stomach started again. She couldn't help wonder if Harry was going to kiss her before he left. Did she want him to? Or was she completely freaked out by the prospect? She dithered, the knot only getting tighter.

Chapter 3

"I'll walk you to the door," Harry offered as he jumped off the bicycle. Hannah considered running inside and closing the door before he could get there. It would take away the whole kiss dilemma. But, then again, half the fun was in the kiss dilemma. She stuck by his side until they reached the porch.

"Thank you for tonight," Hannah started, smiling because she still couldn't stop. "I think it was fantastic for our first official date."

"Me too. Besides the getting soaked part."

"Even the getting soaked part." She looked up at him, seeing the cheeky sparkle in Harry's eyes. He looked adorable, even with his matted hair as it clung to the side of his face. She really wanted to be brave enough to brush it back but she wasn't – yet. She let the hair cling there.

An awkward silence lingered between them. Hannah's heart was beating so fast she wondered if it was going to break a rib or two. Or several. It hammered in her chest, unrelenting.

Hannah couldn't take it any longer. "I guess I should go inside. Are you working at the shelter tomorrow?"

"Yeah, tomorrow morning. You?"

"Yeah, in the morning." She watched as he nodded slowly, his mind clearly elsewhere. She took a step towards the door, her hand reaching for the handle. Obviously her question was answered – they wouldn't kiss. "Thanks again."

"No, wait," Harry stopped her, placing his own hand over hers so she wouldn't turn the door handle. He leaned in quickly, like he would change his mind if he moved too slowly.

Their lips collided. It wasn't exactly the most passionate of kisses, but it was sweet… and perfect. Hannah closed her eyes and tried to turn off her mind. But there it was, stressing out about if she was kissing correctly. Was her breath okay? What should she do with her free hand? Should she be the first one to pull away? The questions wouldn't stop for the entire duration of the kiss.

Finally, Harry let her go. "See you tomorrow."

She leaned against the door and watched him leave. With a simple wave, he disappeared down the street and out of her sight. Her heart was even worse as she opened the door and went inside.

"You're back early," Coco called from the living room. She turned around and got a look at Hannah for the first time. "What happened to you?"

"A wave happened."

Coco just shrugged, no further explanation was

needed. "Did you have a good time?"

Hannah considered brushing her mother off with a simple, one syllable answer, but she couldn't. She was too wired to just go to bed, she wanted to talk. "I had the best time ever. He had a picnic waiting for us on the beach. We ate by moonlight and it was so perfect. I feel like I'm so lucky to be treated that way by a guy, I can hardly believe it."

Coco rushed over, giving her all her attention. "I am so glad to hear that. You deserve someone that treats you like a queen. Anything less and you shouldn't be with them."

"I just can't get over why he likes me so much," Hannah confessed. She had been over it so many times in her head. Why did Harry choose to be with her when he could get any girl he wanted? She didn't see there was anything special about her. Quite the opposite, in fact, she was boring and plain.

"Why he likes you so much? Because he knows quality when he sees it." Coco took her daughter's hands in her own, looking directly into her eyes to get the message across. "You are a wonderful, beautiful, smart, young woman. Any guy would be lucky to know you. Don't ever think you're not good enough for someone. It's more likely that they aren't good enough for *you*."

"You're just saying that because you have to. You're my mom."

"No, I'm not. I'm saying it because it's true. The sooner you realize that, the better you'll be."

Hannah still wasn't sure if she believed it or not. But she wasn't going to argue with her mother – there was no use. Instead of fighting, she just gave her mom a tight hug. "Thanks, Mom."

"You're welcome, my baby girl. Now go and change before you catch a cold or something."

She let her go and Hannah went upstairs, keen on a shower and some sleep. She couldn't get their date out of her mind, all the good bits kept replaying over and over again. It was perfect in every way – just like Harry. She couldn't wait to tell Veronica all about it.

By mid-morning the next day, Hannah was still smiling about their date. She tried to hide it from Harry, but he caught her on several occasions grinning to herself and looking off into space.

"We've got another missing dog," Cory said as she came into the washing area. "That makes two today. What's going on with all the owners lately? It's not that hard to keep an eye on your pet."

Hannah rinsed off the Golden Retriever she was washing. He was actually enjoying the bath, unlike most of the other dogs. "How many dogs normally go missing?" She asked, worried.

"Maybe one or two a month," Cory replied, waving the missing animal reports around as she spoke. "We usually have the pets here too or they're found pretty quickly. There's normally only a handful that never get found. If this keeps up, I'm going to go crazy."

She stomped off to her office and slammed the door behind her, making both Hannah and the Golden Retriever jump.

"She's not grumpy with us," Hannah soothed, speaking baby talk to the dog before pulling the plug on the water. "She's just grumpy. Now shake."

Right on cue, the dog shook all the water everywhere. Only some of it found its way onto

Hannah. She was smarter now; she always held a towel in front of herself before she pulled the plug. She wasn't going to get herself drenched again.

Harry brought in the next dog and she started washing the little mixed breed that was fluffy and white – and cunning. Hannah knew this particular dog liked to jump out of the tub at every opportunity she got.

As she scrubbed her with a soapy sponge, Hannah couldn't get her mind off all the missing dogs. It was so sad that the animals weren't safely with their family. They would be fending for themselves, out in the world without their home or loved ones. It broke her heart to think about it.

"Hey, Harry," she started, getting his attention away from the kitten he held in his arms. "I think we need to do something about the missing dogs. Someone needs to do something about it and it may as well be us."

"I was thinking the same thing," Harry agreed, absentmindedly stroking the little cat. She purred under his touch.

"I'm beginning to believe you might have been on the right track last night when you said someone might be taking them."

He nodded sadly. "It looks that way. There's too many for it to be a coincidence."

"Do we tell the police?"

"They won't care."

Hannah knew he was right. There was no evidence, it wasn't like it was a life or death situation, and the police force would be busy with other things. The likelihood of them doing anything about it was slim to none.

"We need some evidence to show them what's going on," Hannah decided. "We're going to have to work it out ourselves."

Harry agreed. When all the dogs were bathed and walked for the day and lunchtime loomed, they retreated into the office intent on doing some investigating.

"Grab the reports," Hannah directed. Harry reached up and pulled down the arch lever file, full of the missing animal reports they had collected over the last few weeks. It was far fatter than it usually was.

She flicked through the reports, trying to find a common thread to the dogs. Were they from the same area? Were they the same breed? What age were they? She needed to see a pattern, something that would give her a clue about their disappearance.

All the animals were from different areas, from one end of town to another. So that couldn't have been the common thread. They were also different ages, but tended to be on the young side. A large number of the dogs were only puppies, but there were some older ones thrown into the mix.

What did stand out for Hannah were the breeds of the dogs. They were all different types, but they were all purebreds. None of the dogs were cross breeds or bits of everything. Each and every one was purchased from a registered breeder with the full paperwork. They were expensive pups, not the type they would normally see wandering the streets lost.

Hannah logged onto the local message boards where people posted items they had for sale. She had a thought that if someone was purposefully taking the dogs, they wouldn't be keeping them. Not unless they had severe animal hoarding problems, anyway.

So what would they do with all those animals? The only option would be to sell them. The dogs were purebreds; they would fetch a pretty penny on the market – especially if they were only puppies.

No matter how many dogs the animal shelter had, people still continued to buy purebred dogs from breeders. Hannah could never figure out why, the ones from the shelter were just as capable of being loved and they would be saving a life. She never understood the attraction of the purebreds.

And those people would probably jump at a bargain if purchased online. Hannah scoured the classifieds, trying to find dogs for sale. There were plenty. Some were litters of puppies – she could discount those. Others were mixes of breeds – those could be ignored. She focused in on the purebred dogs, the ones they were only too happy to list in the ads.

"I think I know this dog," Hannah said as she pointed to one of the ads. She scrambled through the reports, trying to find the one she recalled.

The ad listed a Chihuahua puppy, only eight weeks old. It was a light tan in colour and male. Hannah found the report she was looking for. Mrs. Mathilde reported her Chihuahua puppy Daisy missing four days ago. He was ten weeks old and went missing from her yard. Most importantly, he was tan in colour.

"What's the chance of that being a coincidence?" Harry asked, amazed at what they had found. He pointed to the next ad. "This one's for a Pug, I'm sure there is a report in the file for a Pug."

He flicked through until he found the one he was

looking for. Sure enough, the details were a match. But, like the Chihuahua, the ad made the dog younger.

"It's probably so people will think they're still a puppy," Hannah explained. "People want young dogs so they can train them better."

"And because puppies are adorable."

Hannah grinned, thinking *he* was extremely adorable for saying that. She tried to focus; it was about finding the dogs, not about how cute and distracting Harry was.

"The contact number for all these dogs are the same," she said, getting back to business. It was bad enough they were sitting so close their arms were touching, she couldn't have her brain muddled up even more. "I think if we find the owner of that number, we're going to find the dogs."

She reached into her pocket for her phone, getting ready to dial. Harry placed his hand over the screen before she could finish the number. "What are you doing?"

"I'm calling the number," Hannah replied simply.

Chapter 4

"You can't just call up someone and accuse them of being a dognapper," Harry said in a panic. "It could be dangerous."

Hannah rolled her eyes; did he really think she was that stupid? "I'm not going to tell him anything. I'm going to call about buying the dog."

"Oh, sorry." Harry removed his hand from her phone sheepishly. He figured it was actually quite a good plan. He waited patiently while Hannah spoke to the person on the phone.

Judging by the look on her face, the conversation didn't seem like it was going very well. She eventually hung up. "The Chihuahua and the Pug are already sold."

"Already? But the ads were only posted in the last few days."

"I told you people liked purebreds, especially cute little ones."

Harry sighed. "So we're back at square one, there's no way to tell if the dogs he sold were the ones that are missing. It's not like he's going to tell us who he sold them to."

"We don't need to know that," Hannah stated, like it should have been obvious. When it was clear he wasn't on the same thought process, she grinned. She liked having all the answers for once while he was in the dark.

"Well? Are you going to tell me or just smile to yourself all afternoon?"

Hannah couldn't let him suffer anymore. "He asked me what kind of a dog I was looking for; I told him I wanted a Dachshund. He took down my number and now we just wait."

Harry finally caught on. "So if someone reports a Dachshund missing and then he calls, we'll know he's kidnapping the dogs."

She nodded. The only part of her plan she didn't like was the fact that the man on the phone could now be stalking the town for a Dachshund puppy that would be taken from its owners. She hoped she was doing the right thing. If things went wrong, she would be making a terrible mistake.

Suddenly, the office door opened. Cory popped her head in. "Remember the kittens, guys, they need to be cleaned out before the end of your shift."

"How could we forget?" Harry replied, already standing. "There's no time like the present."

Hannah put the report folder away and replaced her phone in her pocket. She would be nervous and anxious until she got that call.

With the amount of kittens they had at the shelter,

it was difficult to stay too worried. Even while they attended to cleaning up their cages, the playful little bundles insisted on attention as they moved about. With every step she took, Hannah had to be sure she wasn't about to step on one of them.

"These kittens are insane," she laughed as one of the tabby cats chewed on her shoelace. It was swatting at it, attacking with vigor. Its little mouth was barely able to reach around the side of her shoe.

"You should fit right in then," Harry teased. He earned a punch on the arm for his effort. "I'm just telling the truth."

"Well, you took me on a date last night so what does that say about you? Are you insane too?"

Harry shrugged, his cheeky grin spread across his face. "Takes one to know one, I guess."

She just rolled her eyes and continued to put down fresh newspaper. To get the paper on the floor, she had to move three kittens and, even then, they wanted to chew on the edges. It was like trying to put an octopus into a string bag, difficult but not impossible.

"Oh, careful," Harry called out quickly, grabbing Hannah by the arm to stop her stepping in the water bowl. It was completely shielded by the newspaper.

She stepped back in surprise, finding herself landing against Harry's chest. "Sorry."

"Don't be." Harry looked down at her, still holding her arm. Suddenly it didn't seem so important to finish cleaning out the kitten cage.

Hannah didn't move, she didn't know if she was still too stunned to or because it just felt good against him. Either way, she wasn't going anywhere. Harry was like a magnet, it was impossible to resist his gravitational pull.

"Guys, the kittens?" Cory said from the doorway. They quickly separated. Hannah could feel her face blushing from being caught together. It wasn't professional.

"Sorry," they both muttered before resuming their cleaning. Cory just laughed; her chuckles could be heard even as she walked down the corridor.

That night, even as she tried to forget about the incident, Hannah was still embarrassed about it. Or perhaps her cheeks continued to redden at the thought of Harry being so close to her. That was a nice memory.

"Hannah, focus, what do think of this outfit?" Veronica clicked her fingers to get her friend's attention before sashaying around in a circle.

"It's nice," Hannah replied, only lying a little. The outfit would have been nice, if there was some more material to it. The skirt was far shorter than she would wear and the top way too low cut for her. Yet somehow Veronica didn't care. And to make it worse, she could completely pull off the entire look. Hannah was both happy for her, and jealous at the same time. "Where is Lucas taking you this time?"

"We're going to the movies and then out for ice cream if we have time. My mother still insists on giving me a ten o'clock curfew so we might have to hurry home." Veronica started on her hair, holding some strands up to experiment with styles.

"Ten o'clock is pretty generous, we're only fifteen."

Veronica stopped, frozen still. "Are you kidding? Are you fifteen or fifty? Sometimes it's like you completely forget you're young."

Hannah shrugged, she was right, sometimes she forgot she was supposed to want to stay out all night. Apparently it wasn't a teenage thing to do to want to go to bed at a reasonable hour.

A part of her really wished she was more like Veronica. It would be so nice to be outgoing and fun, even if it was only for one day. Hannah had tried it once. She woke up one morning and told herself she was going to be different. She was going to do whatever she felt like, regardless of the consequences.

The outcome? She was forced to stay back in Geography class when she tried to leave early. More time with Mr. Shapiro and his dusty world globes was punishment enough. The lesson Hannah learnt was that she couldn't change who she was and perhaps that was a good thing. At least the normal Hannah didn't end up in detention. That kind of behavior wouldn't look good on her college applications.

"You know what we should do?" Veronica asked excitedly, bringing Hannah crashing back to reality. She shook her head, dreading what she could possibly say. "We should totally double date now."

"I don't know…"

"You promised. You said once you and Harry had been on an actual date, you'd come out with Lucas and me. You said it yourself." She stood with her perfectly manicured hands on her hips.

Hannah couldn't do anything but cave under the glare. She *did* say something like that. "Fine. But I'll have to check with Harry and see if he wants to first."

"Of course he will, if he knows what's good for him."

Hannah's phone rang, interrupting them. She

answered, relieved of the reprieve. "Hello?"

"Are you still looking to buy a Dachshund?" The male voice was straight to the point. Hannah sat up, on full alert. This was one phone call she didn't want to stuff up.

"Yes, do you have one?" Veronica gave her a questioning look, she waved her away.

"Yeah. Meet me in Hanson Park tomorrow at ten o'clock. It will be one hundred and fifty dollars."

"How will I know who you are?"

"I'll find you." He hung up without saying anything else. Hannah just stared at her phone.

"Who was that?" Veronica asked, trying to put all her discarded outfit choices back in her overflowing closet.

"It was a man about a dog."

"You're getting a dog?"

"It's a long story," Hannah answered. Suddenly a double date didn't seem nearly as scary as meeting a stranger in the park about a dog. She just hoped her instincts were right.

Chapter 5

The nerves and anxiety were only getting worse the next morning as ten o'clock approached. Hannah was trying desperately to keep herself occupied so she couldn't think of her meeting but it was virtually impossible. Even hosing out the empty cages reminded her of the dog she was going to attempt to buy.

"You know, if it's not what we think it is," Harry started. "You're going to have a dog."

"Don't say that, my mom would kill me if I brought a dog home. She doesn't do pets, she's made that painfully clear throughout my entire childhood," Hannah insisted. She had lost count of how many times she had asked for a cat or a dog. Even a goldfish would have done. Every time, Coco had shot down her request. She always said the same thing: children were enough of a handful. "Is it wrong to want the dog to be stolen so we can return it to its owner?"

"And avoid your mom's wrath? Yeah, it's probably okay." Harry grinned that adorable smile he had but it only slightly made her feel better.

The bell rung from the front reception counter, grabbing both their attention. "I'll get it," Harry offered. He dropped his wet sponge, dried his hands on his shorts, and left her there. She continued with the hose, determined to focus on only her tasks.

Eight minutes later, Harry returned, holding another missing animal report in his hand. "You're never going to guess what just got reported as missing."

Hannah suspected she knew exactly what it was. "Let me guess, a Dachshund?"

Harry nodded. "I guess you don't have to worry about taking home a dog today after all."

While that was a relief, it wasn't Hannah's main concern. "We need to tell Cory what's going on."

"She might stop us meeting with the guy."

"He might be dangerous, I'd feel better if someone knew what we were up to," she confessed. If there was anything drilled into her growing up, it was that adults needed to know what was going on. The last thing Hannah wanted to do was to get herself into something she couldn't get herself out of. And meeting with a dognapper was right up that alley.

They found Cory in her office and reeled off everything they had discovered. She listened to the whole story before she said anything, just nodding her head in the interim.

"And you think this man will sell you the stolen Dachshund today?" She finally asked. They both nodded in response. "Do either of your parents know

30

about this?" This time, they shook their heads. "You could be doing something very stupid."

"We know," Hannah replied. "But we didn't think the police would believe us so we thought if we found some evidence…"

"With evidence we could show them exactly what's happened so they would take us seriously," Harry finished.

Cory studied them both, considering everything they had told her. She pouted her lips, deep in concentration. Just when they thought she was going to forbid them, she spoke. "You are going to need to wear a microphone so we can record the conversation."

"So you'll let us do it?" Hannah asked in shock. It wasn't the response she was really expecting – only hoping for.

"I'll come with you so I can supervise but I'm going to deny knowledge of it all if your parents ask. I would rather deal with a dognapper than parents. Okay?"

"Deal."

Cory pulled down a box from the top shelf of her desk and opened it. Inside were a bundle of wires. She pulled at one, teasing it out of the knot until it was free. She handed over the microphone. "We use these for suspected abuse cases. Put this on and make sure it can't be seen."

Hannah accepted the wire. On one end was a small microphone on a clip and on the other was a black box, presumably to record the voices. She knew from movies she had seen that the box clipped onto your pants at the back while the wire snaked up and around to be taped to your chest. She picked up some tape and headed out the back.

She struggled to get it right. It was difficult holding up her top with one hand and getting the wire in the sticky tape with the other. Harry couldn't watch her any longer.

"Let me help you," he offered, grabbing the tape. She let him take the wire and held up her top as much as she was comfortable with.

She held her breath as he reached around and tucked in the box, taping the wire at intervals as he brought it around to her stomach and started moving upwards. His fingers tickled, sending out tingles of warmth wherever he touched her bare skin.

She could feel his breath on her skin he was so close. She tried not to notice, desperately trying to keep the blushing out of her cheeks. He was just doing a job, just attaching the microphone so they could gather evidence. Nothing more. Yet she was still acutely aware of how close he was to her.

"You might want to do this last bit," Harry said, holding up the microphone. He had reached her ribcage and the edge of her top. Hannah wasn't entirely sure, but she thought he might be blushing himself just a little.

"Thanks," she replied. She slipped the microphone up underneath her top and nestled it into her bra. With one last piece of tape, she secured it in place. "Can you see it?" She asked without thinking, forgetting she was actually asking Harry to look at her chest.

He glanced quickly. "I think it's hidden. Does it feel alright?"

"I think so."

"Are you sure you still want to do this?" He looked

at her with concern; it only made her smile at his worry for her. It was sweet. "You can still back out, I can take your place."

"I'm the one he's been talking to, I'll be fine. You and Cory will be watching me. If anything happens, you'll be there in two seconds."

"We will be," Harry assured her resolutely. She didn't doubt it for even a moment. They would have her back; they wouldn't let anything happen to her. "You're going to need this too."

He pulled out a wad of cash, the asking price of one hundred and fifty dollars. She hadn't even thought of how they were going to pay for the dog, she scolded herself for not thinking about it sooner.

"I can't take your money," she insisted.

"Just take it, we'll get it back when the guy is arrested."

"You might not get it back."

"Hannah, just take it." He held out the money, refusing to take it back. She didn't like it but didn't see any other option. She knew Harry came from a family that could afford it, but she didn't want to take advantage of him. She normally never even thought about the difference in their family's earnings.

"Thank you. I'll try to make sure you get it back," she promised. "We should get going, it's almost ten o'clock. I don't want to be late."

Harry agreed. He gathered up Cory and she drove them to Hanson Park. She parked a discrete distant away. Far enough so they couldn't be noticed, close enough to see what was going on.

Hannah got out and walked into the park by herself. She held the money in an envelope nervously, her sweaty fingers gripping it tightly. If the guy didn't show soon, she thought for sure she would have a heart attack before they could meet.

"Hannah?" The male voice came from behind. She spun around, seeing a short and stocky guy in his twenties. His hair was closely shaven in a buzz cut and he spoke with a slight lisp. He didn't seem like the criminal mastermind she was expecting.

"Yes, that's me," she replied, trying not to let her nerves show. "Are you the one selling the Dachshund puppy?" He didn't have a dog with him, but she knew she didn't know him from anywhere else. The knot in her stomach got worse.

"I am. Do you have the money?"

"Where's the puppy?"

"In the car, I'll bring him over after I'm paid," he said, standing a bit too close for comfort. His eyes kept moving, darting everywhere but on her face.

"You said one hundred and fifty?" She didn't know whether she should give him the money without seeing the dog. Was he just scamming her? Did the dog even exist? She wondered whether she had stumbled over an entirely different scam than they had first thought.

"That's right."

"I want to see the dog first," Hannah demanded, as politely as possible. She didn't want to make him mad but didn't want to just hand over Harry's money on a promise from a dodgy stranger either. "How will I know if I love him if I haven't seen him?"

"He's cute, you're going to love him. The money first and then I'll get him."

He didn't seem like he was going to budge. He was clearly much better at negotiations than she was.

Hannah was painfully aware of that fact. She handed him the envelope, silently praying he would keep his end of the bargain. "It's all there. I want to take him now."

"Wait on the seat over there and I'll go get him." He nodded towards a park bench sitting underneath a tree.

"Don't be too long, I need to get home," Hannah said, hoping she wouldn't be sitting there all day and he wouldn't turn up. The Dachshund had been reported missing; he had to have the dog. Perhaps one of the scams was selling him to a few different people and giving him to only one? It was entirely possible.

She sat on the bench as directed and waited. Out of the corner of her eye she could see Harry and Cory in the car, wondering what she was doing. She gave them a slight nod of her head to reassure them. To anyone else watching her, it would have just seemed like she was scratching her nose. They understood the signal though and stayed in the car.

Hannah waited. And waited. As each moment passed, the knot grew impossibly tight. So tight that she wondered whether it would ever be unraveled.

Chapter 6

Hannah wondered how long she should sit in the park and wait for the guy to return with her Dachshund puppy. How long should it take for her to completely lose hope and realize she had made a big mistake? Ten minutes? Twenty? Forty? It was going on fifteen minutes and it already seemed too long to wait.

She started to stand; clearly he wasn't going to come back. She slowly headed back to the car, her head hanging in disappointment. She didn't know what she was going to say when she got back to the others.

"Hey! Where are you going?" She turned around to see the man hurrying towards her. Her heart leapt. Under his left arm was a dark brown Dachshund puppy, his tail wagging.

Hannah ran over to him, accepting the dog from his arms. "He's adorable."

"He's all yours. You have my number, if you know of anyone else that wants a dog, pass it along."

"I will, thank you." She watched him leave, holding the puppy against her chest. He licked her neck as his tail moved frantically. He was gorgeous, it was definitely love at first sight. She had to keep reminding herself that she wasn't going to keep him. The puppy belonged to someone else and she was going to reunite them. That would be a wonderful feeling too.

Only when the guy was completely out of sight did Hannah return to the car. She climbed in as Cory started the engine and took off. They didn't want to wait around for the man to see any of them.

"I think he likes you," Harry laughed. The puppy gnawed on Hannah's fingers, the entire time his tail did not stop. He was starved of attention, that was for sure.

"I like him too," she replied, unable to take the smile off her face. She had seen some cute puppies before, especially in the shelter, but the little Dachshund was adorable. Obscenely cute and cuddly with his short legs.

"I've called the woman who reported him missing," Cory said, the voice of reason from the front seat. "She's going to meet us at the shelter."

Hannah was sad to hear she wouldn't have much time with the puppy, but she knew he would be overjoyed at going home to his rightful owner.

When they entered the shelter, the woman was already there and pacing with anticipation. Harry stood with his hand on Hannah's back, letting her know he was there for her. She appreciated his support, but she was okay with handing over the puppy. She knew it would come to this.

Cory greeted the woman; she didn't seem interested

in small talk. "You said you had my puppy."

"We think we do," Cory replied, she nodded for Hannah to step forward. "Is this your dog?"

Hannah held him up, trying to see the look of recognition on the dog's face when he spotted his owner. Yet he seemed indifferent. Perhaps it was just because he was a puppy? Maybe she didn't own him for very long before he was dognapped?

"That's not my puppy," the woman stated bluntly. The three exchanged a glance.

"Are you sure?" Harry asked.

"Of course I'm sure, I know my own dog. Maxie has a small white patch on his muzzle. This dog doesn't, he's not mine. You said you had my dog."

"I said we *might* have your dog," Cory corrected her, trying to calm her down. "It seems we'll need to keep looking for Maxie."

"Don't get my hopes up again." She stomped out before they could say anything else.

"She was charming," Hannah said sarcastically. But she couldn't be insulted, not when she had an adorable little puppy in her arms. She stared into his chocolate brown eyes, completely smitten. Until something occurred to her. "If this isn't her puppy, I'm going to have to take him home."

"He's only young, it wouldn't be a good idea to keep him here," Cory warned. "He needs overnight attention or he'll upset all the other dogs."

"My mom's going to kill me," Hannah groaned. She was already imagining the situation. Coco would freak out, she'd beg to allow him to stay, they'd have a fight, they'd probably both cry and storm off to their respective bedrooms, and slam the door. It wasn't going to be pretty.

"Do you want me to come with you?" Harry asked, sitting on his bicycle and waiting to leave the shelter.

"No, I'll be fine," Hannah replied, hoping she wasn't lying. She had the puppy tucked down her shirt so she could grip both the handlebars. He seemed happy enough for the short ride. "Don't forget our double date tonight."

"How could I?" He grinned cheekily before racing off. She did the same in the opposite direction. She was dreading going home but it had to be done. If she procrastinated too long, she wouldn't have time to get ready for her date.

As she walked in through the front door, Hannah seriously considered smuggling the puppy in and hiding him in her room. If she didn't have plans to go out that night, she might have done it too. But she couldn't leave the puppy by himself all night; it wouldn't be fair to him. And if Coco heard noises coming from her room, she would only go snooping.

"Mom, I'm home."

"Good, I have an early dinner for you. I don't want you being late for your big date." Coco joined her in the hallway. She stopped in her tracks when she spotted the Dachshund. "What's that?"

"A puppy. I need to look after him but it's only going to be for a short time. I promise I'll do everything, you won't even know he's here," she said quickly and without taking a breath. She gasped for air afterwards.

"You know I don't like pets in this house."

"He's just a puppy, I couldn't leave him at the shelter. He's lost so we're trying to find his real parents."

Coco shook her head in exasperation. "And who's going to look after him when you go out tonight?"

Now it was time for some serious convincing. "I don't think I tell you enough how much I love you, you know that? You're the best mom in the whole, entire world."

She rolled her eyes. "I know what you're doing, don't think I'm that gullible. But I guess I'll look after it tonight, but just tonight. That thing is your responsibility."

Hannah threw her arms around Coco's neck and gave her a quick hug. "Thank you, thank you, thank you. I promise he won't be any trouble."

"It better not be or you'll be coming home early."

It was enough permission Hannah needed. She gave the puppy some of the food she brought home from the shelter before having her own dinner. She quickly got ready for her date and made sure he had a walk outside. She was already falling in love with the little thing. With each minute that passed, she knew it was going to be even harder to hand him back.

She left the dog with Coco on the lounge as Harry picked her up. She was getting used to riding on his handlebars and quite skilled at the kind of balance she needed to accomplish not falling off. Most of all, she enjoyed snuggling against his chest for the whole ride.

Veronica and Lucas were waiting for them as they arrived at the cinemas. Hannah was instantly nervous. She knew Veronica was more outgoing and no doubt way more confident with Lucas than she was with Harry. Would he wish for her to be like that too? Would he think she was a bad girlfriend for being more reserved? Anxiety was gripping her, threatening to direct her legs to run in the opposite direction.

"So, we're seeing Sweet Revenge, it's a romantic comedy. Any objections?" Veronica announced, looking down the boys. They, like Hannah, didn't dare to object. They towed the line, following her to the ticket booth and then into the cinema.

Hannah sat between Harry and Veronica. She was all too aware of Harry's arm resting close to her own. As the lights dimmed and the previews started, she stared at his hand. She would have liked to hold it with her own. They could sit there in the dark and just have that secret connection without anyone else knowing. Yet she just couldn't bring herself to do it. Even after seeing Veronica holding Lucas's hand in the shadows.

The movie could have been good but Hannah wasn't entirely paying attention. She was too caught up in seeing what everyone else was doing. From her seat, she could see a few other couples. She wished she could be as at ease as they were.

To make it worse, she didn't even know why she was so anxious around Harry. She spent nearly every day with him at the shelter and everything was fine. But the moment she was in a social situation, she just tensed up. It was like she put way too much pressure on herself to be a normal girlfriend – whatever that was. She knew she had to relax but didn't know how.

By the time the movie ended, Hannah was relieved. She wondered if it was always going to feel this way, always be this difficult. She hoped not. In all the movies it looked easy but she knew she wasn't a normal girl. Perhaps awkward was how she was always going to be.

"Do you want to get some ice cream? I think we have time," Veronica asked. Harry immediately looked at Hannah to see what she wanted to do.

She felt trapped and her natural instincts were to say no. "It's getting late and it's been a long day. Maybe another time?"

"Plus, you have a puppy to look after," Harry added happily. It was sweet, she could tell by the disappointment in his eyes that he wasn't really ready to leave. Yet she couldn't get out of her mood. Hannah needed to go home and think about things, she was no good to anyone.

"You got a puppy?" Veronica asked, scandalized. "How did you convince your mom?"

"I'm not keeping it, just looking after him for a few days. Trust me, I'm sure I'm going to hear all about it when I get home."

"Come on." Harry patted her on the back. "I'll take you home and shield you from anything she throws at you."

Hannah smiled, he really was so sweet. She wished she was a better girlfriend, he certainly deserved better. They rode home and Harry only left after she convinced him Coco's bark was worse than her bite.

She entered the house, expecting to hear every part of how inconvenienced Coco was by the puppy. He probably went potty inside the house, barked when he shouldn't have done, and chewed on the cushions or something. No matter what the poor little puppy did, she would no doubt complain about it.

"Mom, I'm home," Hannah sighed, heading for the living room where the television was on.

"Oh, you're early." She turned around with a weird

look on her face, like she had just been caught doing something she shouldn't have been doing.

Hannah noticed but continued anyway, not sure if she wanted to know. "How was the puppy?"

She went around the lounge to sit next to her, finally seeing exactly what Coco was up to. The puppy was asleep on his back, all four of his short legs up in the air while he was being cradled in her arms. She was babying the poor thing and he didn't seem to mind at all.

"He's been such a good little baby-waby," Coco replied in baby talk. It was worse than Hannah had expected – her mother had bonded. "I gave him a name, it's Bubbie. Don't you think it suits him? He's my little Bubbie."

"Mom," Hannah whined. "We have to give him back when we find out who his real owner is. We can't name him and fall in love. He's not ours."

Hurt crossed her face as she pouted. "Can't we keep him?"

"No, he doesn't belong to us."

"But he's so cute and he loves me."

Hannah rolled her eyes. "I thought you hated dogs, you never let me get one when I was growing up."

"They were never this cute."

Hannah laughed, already wondering how she was going to wrangle the puppy out of her mother's arms.

Chapter 7

The next day, Hannah was still feeling melancholy. Even the cute little kittens couldn't cheer her up. She was troubled about not being good enough to be Harry's girlfriend. Like one day he would realize that and it would only be a matter of time before he broke her heart. Seeing the way Veronica and Lucas acted together was completely different to her and Harry. She still couldn't help but wonder why he was so nice to her.

"Hannah," Cory said, getting her attention. "These lovely people want to buy a kitten."

Hannah plastered on a smile, it was amazing what you could hide with one of those. "Of course, we have plenty of them."

Cory turned back to the couple. "Hannah will help you pick out the perfect pet. You're in great hands."

She took the couple from Cory and led them to the kitten cages. There were dozens of kittens to choose from in every color available. Each one had their own little personality and spirit. Hannah hated to see any of them leave, but it would make her so happy to know they were with a family that loved and cared for them.

"Feel free to pick them up and play until you find the one that belongs with you," she said while giving them some space to bond. She lingered nearby in case they had questions or they made their decision. The couple seemed nice, they played with most of the kittens, petting and cuddling them.

"I think it's come down to one of these two," the woman finally said, holding up two of the baby cats. One was a ginger stripe, the other a little grey. "Which one would you recommend?"

Hannah had no idea, they were both adorable. She had a better idea though. "Why don't you take both? Kittens are really social, they love having a playmate. If a single cat is left alone for too long they can get really bored. You'll be saving your furniture by taking two."

The woman exchanged a glance with her partner. Hannah couldn't believe they were actually considering it. She always tried to talk people into taking two so the little kitten wouldn't be lonely; people rarely took her up on the offer.

"It's up to you, Babe," the guy answered. The woman stood, still holding both the ginger and the grey kittens.

"Two kittens won't be any more trouble than one," the woman shrugged, like she was trying to convince herself. "And they *would* get lonely if we only had one."

Hannah held her breath while she dithered. She didn't want to say anything else in case she talked her out of the decision.

With one decisive nod, the woman made up her mind. "We'll take both." All three of them grinned, none more so than Hannah. She took them through to reception and handed them back over to Cory to do the paperwork.

It was hard saying goodbye to the little kitties, but the couple were going to take good care of them. Hannah knew they would be happy. Every pet belonged in a family and now two were going to be smothered with love.

She found her mood lifting; it was hard to stay sad when she had just created a family. She heard Harry arrive for his shift, she reflexively checked her watch – he was almost an hour late. He was never late for his shift.

"Sleep in through your alarm this morning?" Hannah teased, a little worried about his tardiness. She knew they were on their summer vacation but Cory still required complete dedication. She was almost as bad as her school principal.

"I wanted to make a detour on the way and it took longer than expected," Harry replied, grimacing a little. "Did Cory notice?"

She had no idea. "I noticed."

He sidled over to her, that cheeky glint in his eyes. She stood still, wondering what he was up to. Before she knew it, he gave her a quick peck on the cheek. It made her blush; despite the way it only made her more embarrassed.

"You're in a good mood," she giggled. It seemed like all the awkwardness from the night before had vanished into thin air.

"How could I not be? I got you a present." He

revealed a small parcel from behind his back.

"Why?"

"Do I need a reason? Because I like you, that's why."

Hannah took the small box, neatly tied with a pink ribbon. Her hands were shaking as she opened it. Inside was a small little square brick that looked like a lump of soap.

"What is it?" She asked, laughing. The whole thing was making no sense whatsoever to her.

Harry picked up the square out of the box and held it up to the light. "It's a towel. When it gets wet, it expands to one hundred times its size. I thought it might come in handy next time we're at the beach having a picnic."

It was the sweetest present she had ever received. Before she could think about it, Hannah threw her arms around him, refusing to let go. "It's perfect, thank you, I love it."

He hugged her back, pulling her so tight she thought she might stop breathing. She couldn't believe she had spent all night worrying about her relationship with Harry. All those countless hours of her just being stupid. It could all have been avoided.

He finally let her go, but only so he could give her a quick kiss on the lips. It was anything but awkward. In fact, it felt so right Hannah wished it wouldn't stop.

"Does this mean we're going on another picnic?" Hannah asked, hoping for a positive answer.

"I think we're going to go on *lots* of picnics," Harry grinned.

The barking of dogs brought them crashing back down to reality as one of the bigger canines knocked over their water bowl. It hurtled over, sending water down to the cage below it.

"I'll get it," Harry offered, letting his arms falls away from her sides before grabbing a mop and bucket. "How did the puppy go last night?"

"My mom is in love. She didn't even let me look after him last night; she took him to sleep in her bed. I hope the real owner comes forward soon or I'll have to smuggle him out of the house."

"I thought she didn't like dogs."

"I did too. She would be very happy if our whole dognapping theory is wrong."

Harry gave her a quick look. "Do you think our theory could be wrong? After all, nobody has reported another Dachshund missing and it's been more than twenty-four hours."

Hannah sighed, she had been wondering the same thing. "If someone isn't kidnapping all the dogs, then it means they're really lost. I can't bear to think of all those lost animals out there on the streets."

"Maybe we could go for a bike ride after our shift?" Harry suggested. "We could look all over for stray dogs?"

"I guess."

"We could get lucky and find them all hanging out at the same place, just hanging around and having a good time."

Hannah giggled, she wished it could be that easy. "I like your optimism."

"Always look on the bright side of life, kid," he said, winking and speaking with a gangster's voice. It only made her laugh harder.

"Hey, kids, get in here," Cory called from the front

reception. They exchanged a glance, hoping they weren't in trouble for something. They hurried through, crossing their respective fingers.

"What is it?" Hannah asked, stopping as she spotted a man with Cory.

"This is Mr. Drysdale," Cory started. "He's missing a Dachshund puppy."

Chapter 8

"My mom's on her way," Hannah said as she hung up her phone. It had taken some convincing but Coco was on her way in with Bubbie. Being able to take him out of her hands was another thing all together.

"How did he go missing?" Harry asked, directing the question at Mr. Drysdale. He was a tall, body builder type of guy. Not quite what you'd expect of a Dachshund owner.

"He was taken from the yard. One minute he was there, the next he was gone. I knew he couldn't get out so I was certain someone had taken him. I only had him a week," he explained.

"And his description matches?" Hannah asked, looking at Cory. She was slightly disappointed they had found Bubbie's owner so quickly, she didn't even get a chance to play with him properly.

"Down to the tee," Cory replied. "Ah, here we are." She indicated to the door as Coco bustled in with

50

Bubbie cradled against her chest. His legs probably hadn't been on the ground since the previous day.

"Rex!" Mr. Drysdale exclaimed. The puppy's tail wagged madly as he lurched for his owner – his real one. Coco let him go reluctantly. Hannah's heart broke for her; she could see the sadness in her eyes already. She was going to be even worse to live with for a while.

"I can't thank you enough for finding him," Mr. Drysdale said, tears sitting in the corner of his eyes. Seeing a grown man dote over a tiny little puppy was certainly something new to Hannah. Her image of body builders worldwide was changed in an instant.

"We're just happy you got him back," Cory said. "Make sure to keep him inside for a while. Only take him outside if you're with him the whole time."

"I'm not letting him out of my sight ever again," he declared. The four of them watched him leave with the little Dachshund.

"I need a coffee," Coco mumbled before storming off.

"So that's your mom," Harry said, teasingly.

"The one and only," Hannah replied. "Now you know why I don't introduce you."

"Thank you."

"You're welcome." She grinned. The best way to describe her mother was always to show them, they instantly understood. Coco spoke for herself.

"Well, kids," Cory started. "We have a dognapper to capture. I'm going to the police to tell them everything. Hold down the fort, I'll be back."

It took her two seconds to grab her handbag and leave them to it. Hannah and Harry returned to their duties, on the edge of their seat until she got back.

The police must have taken her seriously because Cory didn't return for over an hour. And when she did, she had two police officers in tow.

They spent the rest of the afternoon going through all the missing dog reports. Hannah and Harry both had to explain everything they had worked out and pass on the details of the man they had brought the Dachshund puppy from.

After receiving a warning for taking the law into their own hands and going into a potentially dangerous situation, the police asked for their help.

"You'll be wearing a hidden camera," the officer explained, he was an older man – in his forties at least. "If anything looks like it's going wonky, we'll get you out of there. Normally we don't get the public involved, especially not a fifteen year old, but you've met with the man already. He trusts you. Do you think you can do it again?"

Hannah didn't even need to think about it. If she could do something to stop all the poor dogs being taken from their owners, she would do it. "I'll do whatever you need me to."

The police officer nodded in acknowledgement. "We're going to need your parent's permission."

"My mom will be fine about it," Hannah replied, wondering if it was actually true or not. Coco was a bit of a drama queen but she normally saw sense eventually. Surely she had to agree? After all, *she* was the one who demanded Hannah do something in the summer break. Thwarting a dognapping ring classified as something, right?

The police finished explaining the plan and then

drove Hannah home, needing to speak with Coco before they could finalize their strategy.

"I don't know, can you guarantee my daughter's safety?" Her mom asked after she had heard the story. She had taken it better than Hannah had expected.

The policeman nodded patiently. "If there is any sign of danger we'll go in immediately. The safety of everyone involved is our highest priority."

"Will she get her name in the paper? Or a bravery medal?"

Hannah could feel her cheeks redden. "Mom, I don't need my name in the paper or a medal. Will you just agree already?"

Coco gave her a warning, silently telling her not to boss her around. She knew the look well, she had received it so many times she was practically immune to its affect.

"Fine, she can do it," Coco finally sighed. "But if she's hurt, I'm going to make you pay for it."

"We'll take care of her," the policeman assured before turning his attention back to Hannah. "We will need you to make a phone call to the man."

"Of course," Hannah replied. They told her exactly what to do before she called the man she had brought the puppy from. This time, she had a friend looking for a purebred Chihuahua. The man agreed to find one for her and hung up. "Now we wait for the call."

Chapter 9

Chihuahuas must be easy to come by, as the man had called back that night. By lunchtime the next day, Hannah was waiting in the park again. Her heart was hammering in her chest as she felt the eyes of the police and Harry on her back.

They weren't just listening to her every word, they could also see what she did. The police had placed a small camera in her handbag, the lens looking like nothing more than a button. She wondered if they were powerful enough to hear her heartbeats.

It was hot standing out under the sun, she wished for some shade or a cool drink. A frozen ice would have been perfect. She made a mental note to get one later, maybe she could go with Harry? She was too lost in her own thoughts to see the man approaching.

"Sorry I'm late," he apologized, reaching her. Instantly she was nervous, fumbling over her words.

"It's... it's okay. You said you found a Chihuahua

puppy for my friend?"

"I do. Do you have the two hundred?"

She nodded and pulled out the wad of cash the police had given her. This time, they were certain of getting the money back. She hoped they would get Harry's back too. "Two hundred dollars, it's all there."

He counted it anyway. "Wait on the bench and I'll get your new dog."

"Thanks." She watched him go; feeling like she'd had the conversation before. Doing as she was told, Hannah waited on the bench. As least it was underneath a leafy tree, the shade was a welcome relief.

The police were doing a good job of hiding. If she didn't know they were there, she wouldn't have even noticed them. Two officers were sitting in the car with Harry and two others were hiding in the trees. None of them were making a sound or movement.

As Hannah waited, she went over the instructions the police had given her. She hoped she didn't forget anything. She didn't want to stuff it all up by doing the wrong thing. She doubted her nerves would take having to go through it all again.

The man returned with a tiny little light brown colored puppy tucked underneath his arm. He walked quickly, ready to get out of there after the transaction was done.

Hannah stood. "She's so cute."

"And all yours. It was nice doing business with you. Remember to tell all your friends about me," the man said happily. He turned to leave and Hannah remembered her cue. She hurried away in the opposite direction. Her instructions were clear: once she had the puppy, she was to get away from the man and return to the car as quickly as possible.

When the car was in sight, Hannah heard a commotion behind her. She turned around just in time to see two policemen tackling the guy to the ground. She now understood why she had to get out of the way – fast.

"You did really well," the police officer greeted her at the car, letting her inside with the puppy. The poor little thing's heart was racing in her chest. She knew how she felt.

"Will he go to jail?" She asked, still nervous about the whole thing. "He's not going to come after me or anything, will he?"

"He doesn't know your address or name, all he has is a phone number. We'll make sure he leaves you alone," he reassured her. She hoped he was right; she'd never been so close to a criminal before. "He'll be locked up for a long time anyway. Thanks to you."

Hannah smiled as Harry patted her on the shoulder, whispering in her ear. "You were awesome."

Never before had she felt prouder. No amount of good grades or right answers on a test gave Hannah the same satisfaction as helping the animals. Everything else paled into comparison when you had just nabbed a criminal.

The police dropped them back at the shelter and ran through everything with Cory. She copied all the missing dog reports for them to take and investigate. Hopefully they would all be found now, with a little help from the man in custody of course.

When all the official business was out of the way, Cory found Hannah and Harry with the dogs. They had just finished feeding them.

Cory leaned in the doorway, regarding them proudly. "You guys did a really good thing."

"Hannah did a really good thing," Harry corrected her.

She tried to suppress the heat threatening to burn her cheeks. "Harry did just as much as I did, we were in it together."

"Well, whoever it was," Cory continued. "I think you deserve a reward. Hannah, considering your mom was so attached to the Dachshund puppy, I think you should adopt a dog. Take any one you like, on the house."

"Seriously?" Hannah asked, incredulous. She didn't care if Coco would approve or not. If she could fall in love with the puppy, she could fall in love with another dog.

"Go for it. I know you'll give it a great home."

"What about me?" Harry asked teasingly.

Cory was out the door as she yelled back. "You can have as many kittens as you like."

Harry and Hannah erupted into laughter. As cute as they were, Harry wanted something a bit more manly than a dozen kittens.

"So which one are you going to choose?" Harry asked, catching his breath again.

Hannah walked up and down the aisles, looking into all the cages. She already loved each and every one of the dogs, it was difficult to choose just one to take home and be a part of their family. She wished she could take them all. Each of them deserved a home.

She finally stopped at the cage of the dog who had been there the longest. He was no breed in particular and reached up to Hannah's knee height. He had been attacked by another animal and found in a terrible state. The vet hadn't given him good odds, but he had fought hard to get back to full health. He was still missing hair in great chunks all over him and his eyes were constantly nervous. Nobody wanted to adopt him, he wasn't pretty enough.

"I'm taking Billy," Hannah decided.

Harry joined her, opening the cage and handing her the dog. "I think Billy is the perfect choice. He's going to be very happy with you and your mom."

Hannah cradled him to her chest, not doubting it for a second. She could already imagine him curling up at the end of her bed, lying on the living room floor in front of the fireplace in wintertime, and running around the backyard with his tongue hanging out.

"My mom's going to freak out."

"So you'll be going home alone today?" Harry grinned.

"Scaredy cat," she teased him.

Chapter 10

Hannah watched as Billy ran around the backyard of her house. She had never seen him happier or more alive. It was like he was a puppy all over again without a care in the world.

"Hannah, you have a visitor," Coco said, stepping aside from the door so she could let him pass.

"Thank you, Mrs. Wilson," Harry said politely. Hannah was instantly in a state of panic. Not only had she not been expecting him, he had been alone with her mother. There were so many things that could have happened in those moments, she didn't even know where to begin.

Coco lingered, grinning to herself as she watched Harry take a seat on the edge of the decking next to Hannah. "Do you want a cold drink, kids?"

"Sure, thanks Mom," Hannah replied, ready to say anything to get rid of her.

As it turned out, introducing Billy to Coco had

been quite easy. Hannah turned up with him and told her his story. By the end of the sad tale, she was sold. That had been almost a week ago and Billy had fit in seamlessly. But he wasn't sleeping on the end of Hannah's bed, he was sleeping on Coco's bed. She barely let the poor thing out of her grip, constantly smothering him with love and affection.

"Billy looks happy," Harry commented, laughing when he picked up a leaf and threw it into the air – only to catch it again. "He's learnt some new tricks too."

"He's like a different dog," Hannah replied. "Just imagine how great it would be if all the dogs at the shelter got adopted."

"I know, right? They could all be having this much fun."

Silence started to threaten them, but it wasn't awkward. Hannah had finally reached the moment when she was just happy to be in Harry's company. They could sit there all afternoon in the sun and she wouldn't care.

"I've been thinking about something," Hannah started.

"Really? I hope it didn't hurt," Harry joked before turning serious. "What's on your mind?"

"You know how I've wanted to be a microbiologist for, like, ever?" She waited until he nodded, glad he was paying attention all those times she'd gone on and on about her future career. "I think I've changed my mind. I want to be a veterinarian. I've been thinking about it long and hard and it just makes sense. I want to help animals, I want to be their voice when they don't have one, I want to make their lives better."

Harry was quiet for so long that she wondered whether she was just being stupid. Finally, he replied. "I think that's a great idea. You will be an awesome vet."

Hannah's heart swelled. "Do you really think so?"

"I know you will." He leaned over and gave her a kiss, one that convinced her she wasn't doing something stupid. She never wanted it to end, cupping his cheek with her hand to make sure it didn't.

"Oh, my," Coco muttered under her breath. They quickly parted.

Hannah thought she might die of embarrassment, her cheeks flaming red. One look at Harry and his rosy cheeks made her forget all about it. They burst into laughter as Coco left the cold drinks for them and retreated back inside.

Harry took a sip, to cool his cheeks just as much as quenching his thirst. "You know, as a future vet, I think you're going to need to spend more time at the animal shelter."

"I think I couldn't agree more," Hannah replied.

She moved closer, letting his arm snake around her back. The sun with shining high in the sky as a cool breeze whispered through the trees. Summer may have been half over, but Hannah felt like her life was only just beginning.

They sat there together, laughing as Billy started to chase a butterfly. He would never catch it but he had a whole lot of fun trying. They were like proud parents as they watched Billy start his new life too.

☙ The End ❧

A Hairy Tail 3

Dedication

For Max.

Chapter 1

Racing through the streets of Mapleton, Hannah felt like she was flying. If she wasn't scared of falling off her bicycle, she would have thrown her arms into the air and let the wind take her along.

She felt better than she had in her entire life. Summer may have been half over, but she had gained a dog, a boyfriend, and more confidence than she had ever had before. It was a perfect summer, one she never wanted to end.

Arriving at the animal shelter, Hannah couldn't believe how happy she was. It was like everything was falling into place and promising a wonderful year ahead. She thought nothing could damage her mood.

The familiar sound of dogs barking and cats meowing filled her ears as she headed towards the back of the Mapleton Animal Shelter. But there was something else too, voices – two of them. One belonged to Harry and another to a female.

Hannah stopped in the doorway, taking in what she was seeing. Harry was talking to a girl, she couldn't have been older than either of them. She was giggling with every word he said. Instantly, Hannah's good mood flitted completely out the window.

"Oh, Hannah, hey," Harry said, taking a step away from the girl. The little movement didn't go unnoticed. "Jessie, meet Hannah."

The girl waved, curling her hair around her other hand. "Hi."

Hannah couldn't speak, she just gave a half-hearted smile back.

"Jessie is volunteering here with us for a while," Harry explained. "She loves animals too, she was just telling me a really funny story about her horses."

"You have horses?" Hannah asked, unable to stop herself. What kind of a person was lucky enough to have not one but multiple horses?

"Just three," Jessie said, like it wasn't a big deal.

"They're all named after Disney princesses," Harry continued, his voice suppressing a laugh. "There's Belle, Aurora, and Snow. Cheesy, huh?"

Jessie playfully pouted. "Don't tease me, I was ten when I named them."

Hannah didn't care if she was ten or five, she didn't like the girl on sight. There was something about her. Or perhaps it was the way she was standing so close to Harry that irked her. Either way, she wished she was dreaming and could just pinch herself to wake up. She tried it, just in case. It only hurt.

"Kids, come in here," Cory called from her office. She sounded distressed. Hannah was just glad of the interruption. Any longer and she may have said something she didn't mean to.

The trio shuffled into Cory's office, seeing it strewn with paperwork. They had never seen it so messy before. Normally Cory was a stickler for organization.

"I've got some bad news," she started. "I thought I could get around it but it has become clear that I can't. Our funding has been cut. The city is making cutbacks across the board to save money. It seems they will no longer be supporting the shelter."

"What? How can they do that?" Hannah asked, instantly outraged. Yet greater than the anger, was her fear. "What's going to happen to the shelter?"

Sadness swept over Cory's face. "We're going to have to close down."

Harry stepped forward. "We can't close, what's going to happen to all the animals?"

"If we don't find them homes…" Cory couldn't bring herself to finish the sentence.

Hannah wasn't going to let anything happen, not if she had something to do with it. "What do we have to do to keep the shelter open? How can we fix this?"

Cory shook her head. "There's nothing we can do, the council won't budge. I've done everything in my power to beg, plead, and negotiate with them. Without money, we don't have a choice."

"Then we find the money," Hannah declared resolutely. "How much do we need?"

"Twenty thousand dollars in the next two weeks or they will force us to close. We can't get that kind of money anywhere."

Harry rubbed his chin, deep in thought, before he spoke. "We can try to raise it. Twenty thousand isn't an impossible amount."

"It sounds like a lot to me," Jessie commented. Hannah shot her a glare, they did not need any negativity in that room. It was full up already.

"We can do fundraising for the money," Hannah continued, unwavering. "If people could see how much good work we do here, they wouldn't want the place to close down. They'll donate, I know they will."

Cory stood, leaning against the desk. "I don't know, guys, it's a lot of money and we only have two weeks. That's not long enough."

"We have to try." Hannah looked at Harry, silently begging for him to agree. "We can't walk away and do nothing. The animals need us. If we don't do this, then who else will? We can't abandon them."

"It's going to be a lot of hard work and we still might not be able to save it," Cory warned them. "Are you sure you're prepared for that?"

"We can do this."

Harry nodded. "Hannah's right, we can do this. Two weeks, twenty thousand dollars, easy. I'm in."

"Me too," Jessie added happily, stealing a glance at Harry.

"Please, Cory, we have to try," Hannah begged. She watched Cory carefully, trying to see her make the right decision.

Finally, she nodded. "Okay. Two weeks, twenty thousand, let's go. Fundraising ideas, I need them now. Throw them at me."

"A bake sale," Hannah offered.

"An open day so people can come and see what we do," Harry added. "They'll have to donate then. We might even get a few adoptions."

"How about a concert? We could get someone

famous to come and sing for us," Jessie suggested. "My dad knows lots of famous people."

Hannah rolled her eyes, of course her father knew famous people. He was probably the king of a small country somewhere too.

Cory jumped on the idea. "That would be fantastic, Jessie, can you ask him?"

"Of course I can."

Chapter 2

Of course Jessie could get her dad to call some famous people. She could get anyone to do anything she liked, Hannah thought to herself as she walked the dogs in the yard. For the first time in weeks, she was doing it by herself. Harry had to teach Jessie how to feed the other animals. Like it was difficult or something.

With each step she took, Hannah grew even more annoyed. Who was Jessie anyway? Just showing up in the middle of summer and taking over the entire shelter, who gave her the right to do that? She was so mad she didn't know how she was going to be able to stand being around her.

She briefly considered leaving the shelter and never coming back. Then she wouldn't have to see Jessie and watch the way Harry looked at her. She wouldn't have to see everyone fawn all over the girl. That would be nice.

But why should she have to? She was there first.

Hannah knew if she left, then Jessie would win. And the last thing she wanted was for Jessie to win. A steely determination filtered through her.

"Come on, pups, we should be getting back," Hannah called to the dogs. They paid her no attention, continuing to run around like wild animals while they were out of their cages. She didn't have the heart to make them hurry back. It wasn't their fault stupid Jessie had turned up at the shelter.

"Who died and made her queen anyway?" Hannah muttered. The dogs just gave her a sympathetic look. She sighed. Being able to cope with Jessie was going to be harder than it sounded. She kept walking.

"My dad knows lots of famous people," Hannah mimicked the girl. She knew she was being petty but really didn't care. "I'm so wonderful and everybody loves me. I'm going to save the shelter single handedly."

"You're going to do what?" Harry asked, sneaking up behind her. She spun around, her face ablaze and red. She didn't know how much he had overheard. Judging by the way his eyes were sparkling with amusement, she guessed quite a bit.

"I, uh, I'm going to round up the dogs and take them back inside," she said, trying to cover her embarrassment. "Are all the others fed?"

"Yeah, they all gave compliments to the chef."

Hannah went to walk past, not wanting to have a conversation with him at the moment. She was too angry and a little of that anger was directed at him too.

He caught her hand, gently stopping her from going any further. "I really liked your bake sale idea. It's traditional, I think it could work."

7

He was just saying that to make her feel better, she just knew it. She wasn't going to fall for it. "I know you like the concert idea better, you don't have to pretend."

"If the concert could be put together in two weeks, then it would raise a lot of money in one go," Harry explained. "But that's a pretty big *if.* I'm not entirely convinced we would be able to do something that big. It would be like putting all our eggs in one basket and crossing our fingers."

Hannah relaxed a little, starting to come around. Perhaps Jessie wasn't as beguiling as she had thought. "You thought it was such a great idea before in the meeting."

He took both of her hands in his, definitively making sure she wasn't going anywhere. "Jessie needs a lot of encouragement to do anything. Her dad is a big shot, if there is any chance he might be able to help, we have to try."

So Harry and Jessie knew each other before that morning, Hannah thought to herself. She couldn't help but wonder just how well they were acquainted. She should have known they were. Everything about Jessie screamed that she was from the hills part of town – just like Harry. The only difference was that Harry was unaffected by his money. She couldn't say the same about Jessie.

Harry continued when she remained silent. "But we also have to try other things too. Just like your bake sale or my open day. We have to do everything we can to keep this place open."

Finally, something Hannah could agree with. "We can't let it close down. All the animals will have nowhere to go."

He nodded, finally letting her hands go as one of the dogs stood at his feet demanding attention. He knelt down, giving the fluffy little thing a good rub behind the ears. She closed her eyes, enjoying the cuddle.

"Oh, I almost forgot," Harry started. "My parents are having a party on the weekend at our place. Would you like to come? You would be saving me from hours of repeating the same conversation over and over again with different people."

Hannah's first reaction was to say no. Meeting Harry's parents, a party, in the rich neighborhood, nothing sounded appealing. The only good part of it all was that she would be there with Harry. Perhaps she could handle it, perhaps she wouldn't shrivel up and die of embarrassment and discomfort.

"Are you sure you want me to come?" She asked, answering a question with a question to buy herself some more time.

"Of course I want you to come. Everything is better when you're around." He said the words so quietly, Hannah wasn't sure she had heard correctly. Still, they brought a smile to her face.

"I'd like to attend, then. Thank you for inviting me," she replied. The beginnings of a knot were already starting to form in her stomach but she pushed it aside for the time being. She had bigger things on her mind to deal with. Like a girl named Jessie.

After putting the dogs back into their cages and finishing her shift, Hannah rode her bicycle home. It wasn't as much fun as the ride to the shelter, but thoughts of Harry still made her happy. She was already trying to think of something to wear to his parent's party. She was going to have to call in expert advice – she would need to ask Veronica for help.

Once inside her front door, bounding feet ran at her. She giggled uncontrollably as Billy welcomed her with endless kisses and tail wags. She collapsed to the ground, surrendering to him. Which only encouraged Billy even further.

"You'll give the poor thing a heart attack," Coco commented, leaning against the wall while she watched the dog go crazy.

"I can't help it," Hannah managed to get out. She grabbed the dog by both hands, pulling him off her so she could stand again. He settled down in her arms.

"Come through, I've made you some cookies for afternoon tea," her mother said as she turned for the kitchen. Hannah followed, letting Billy down when he could control himself. "How was the shelter today?"

"A new girl started."

"That's good, you have another set of hands to help. What's she like? Does she go to your school?"

Hannah didn't even know where to begin. "Her name is Jessie and she's just perfect. She knows Harry." She slumped onto a stool, hunching over the cookies. She figured she could probably eat the entire batch and still not feel better.

Coco could tell Jessie wasn't exactly a welcome addition. "I take it you don't like her?"

"Harry likes her."

"Oh, Honey, Harry's a nice kid. I'm sure he's not the kind of boy to hurt you like that."

Hannah wasn't so sure. She had never had a boyfriend before, she didn't know what they could do to hurt you yet. "What do I do, Mom? She's going to ruin everything. I don't even want to go back there again."

"You know what really bugs girls like that?" Coco asked, waiting for her daughter's full attention before going on. "Become their best friend. Be as nice to this Jessie as you can be. She'll wonder what on Earth is going on. She'll be too confused to do anything to you."

"You really think that will work? What about Harry? I don't want to lose him."

"He'll see that you're making an effort to be nice to his friend and he'll love you all the more for it. It's a win-win situation."

Hannah shoved an entire cookie into her mouth and chewed. Perhaps her mother wasn't as clueless as she thought.

Chapter 3

"They look like they're ready," Veronica said, peering into the oven. "Hand me the oven mitt." Hannah picked up the glove and did as she was told, making space on the kitchen bench for the trays.

Carefully, Veronica pulled the four trays from the oven and placed them on the bench. Four dozen cupcakes stared at them, begging to be iced when they were cooled. "Do you think this is enough?"

Veronica shrugged. "It's a start. If these sell, we can make more and increase the price." Hannah giggled, she was going to make an excellent businesswoman one day. "How many would we need to save the shelter?"

"Let's see, at two dollars a cupcake, less the cost of ingredients, about thirteen thousand," Hannah said, doing the math in her head. "But every dollar counts so I still think it's worth doing."

"And you want to prove Jessie wrong."

"That too," she agreed. They said the bake sale wouldn't be a good way to raise funds, but Hannah was certain neither was relying on a single concert to save them. She had to try to fundraise in her own way, every dollar contributed to keeping the shelter doors open. Do enough small things and they always added up to something big.

They iced the cupcakes in pink as soon as they were cool enough and packed them into plastic tubs – careful not to damage the stock.

Coco dropped them off at the supermarket and they set up a stall outside. Hannah surveyed the table, with the cupcakes and posters she made, it looked professional enough. She just hoped people were hungry and in a generous mood. The stall wasn't just about selling the cupcakes, she was asking for donations too.

Her and Veronica stood at the stall, trying to lure people over for a tasty treat. "It's to keep the Mapleton Animal Shelter open. They have lost their funding and we need help to look after all the homeless animals," she called out repeatedly anytime someone walked past.

One hour into the bake sale and they had sold about a dozen of the cupcakes. It was difficult keeping the stall in the shade to avoid spoilage in the hot summer sun. They had to move the table several times.

"Oh, hey, you went ahead with the bake sale." Hannah heard the sweet voice before she looked up. She already knew it belonged to Jessie. "I'll take two, they look really good."

"Hi Jessie," Hannah finally greeted her. Coco's voice replayed in her mind, she needed to be friends with her. Unfortunately, that was easier said than done. "You aren't working today?"

"I was there this morning. Harry was too. We missed you."

"I normally don't work Tuesdays, Harry doesn't usually either."

"Harry's so sweet," Jessie gushed, handing over the four dollars. "He wanted to make sure I could handle it there by myself so he spent a few hours with me."

"Kind of defeats the purpose of being on your own, doesn't it?" Hannah asked, keeping her voice teasing like she didn't really mean it. Except she did.

Jessie shrugged. "Work is always more fun when you have someone there with you, right? I always find that, anyway."

Veronica shot Hannah a look, silently questioning whether this was *the* girl. "Oh, I uh, forgot to introduce you two. Jessie, this is my best friend Veronica. Veronica, this is Jessie, she's helping out at the shelter for a while."

They nodded a *hey* to each other before Jessie said: "Not just for a while, Hannah, for the rest of the summer. I'm completely committed to doing my civic duty."

"We have you for the rest of the summer? That's great," Hannah lied. She plastered on a smile, making it seem as real as possible. She was certain it probably looked as fake as it felt.

"Oh well, I should keep going," Jessie said, picking up her two cupcakes. "These look really yummy. Good luck with the sale, Hannah. It was lovely to meet you, Veronica."

"You too," Veronica replied. The two girls watched

Jessie bounce away happily, taking a bite out of one of the cupcakes. "She seems nice."

"Not you too."

"I mean, she's horrible. How can you even put up with her around?"

Hannah grinned. "That's more like it."

They remained outside of the supermarket until each and every cupcake had been sold. Hannah was determined to ensure her fundraising plans were going to work. Every dollar counted. If everyone did something small, it would add up to something big. Relying on a single concert to save the shelter was risky and she didn't believe in risks.

By the time it was her shift at the shelter two days later, Hannah was confident she was right. She just wasn't going to be telling anyone else about the funds she was raising. They would only laugh at her.

Harry was in Cory's office, Hannah passed by and stopped, not used to seeing him there. "Hey, what are you doing in here?"

His head shot up to see her, instantly relaxing into a grin. "I've been going through the books for Cory. I think we can cut down on a lot of the costs so we can survive on less money each year."

Hannah joined him, looking over his shoulder. "You really think so?"

"Numbers are kind of my thing," Harry confessed. "I know this will work. All I have to do is make a few phone calls and I'll be able to get better deals."

"That's great news."

She left him to the books, keen to distance herself from the accounting ledgers. She much preferred the company of the kittens. They were all completely oblivious to the financial troubles of the shelter.

She started cleaning out the cage, doing her best to avoid stepping on any of the little fur balls. They were as playful and lively as ever. Some of them were also getting big. If they weren't adopted soon, they wouldn't be kittens anymore. It would be even more difficult to find homes for grown cats.

Just as playtime commenced and all the hard work was done, Harry emerged from the office to join her. He picked up a handful of kittens, sitting on the ground next to Hannah. "We can't close the shelter, where else could we play with kittens all day?"

Hannah smiled. "I know, right? Maybe we could just charge people to cuddle the kittens, then they would get the cuteness without the responsibility."

"That's an idea."

They fell into silence, the only sound being an occasional *meow* from their feline friends. Harry noticed. "Is everything alright?"

"Yeah, why wouldn't it be?"

"I don't know, you're just quieter than usual."

Hannah shrugged, not wanting to get into it. She didn't even know how to mention what was bothering her. "I guess I'm just worried about this place."

He patted her back in comfort. "Me too. But the concert is going to solve everything. We're going to raise enough money, I just know it. Jessie's dad is getting someone really big for us. Jessie told me all about it last night."

"What happened to not putting all your eggs into one basket?"

"I guess I'm just really excited about the concert."

"I don't think we should-" She was cut off as Jessie

poked her head through the door from the dog area.

"Harry, I can't remember what the mix of food is for the dogs. Would you show me one more time?" She asked, looking directly at Harry and only Harry. Apparently Hannah was invisible. "Please?"

"Sure," he answered, getting up. He left Hannah alone with the kittens. She figured she should start getting used to it, it was happening more and more as the days went on.

The bell from reception rang and Hannah went to answer it, knowing Harry wouldn't be able to tear himself away from Jessie to deal with it.

Veronica was standing at the counter. "What are you doing here?"

"I thought I might come in and say hi, see all these cute animals you're always going on and on about," Veronica said happily. In her sandals and pretty white dress, she wasn't exactly dressed for an animal shelter but Hannah didn't care. She wasn't going to be alone for a while.

"Come on through," she said, leading her back. They started with the kittens before moving onto the dogs. Jessie and Harry were outside, exercising the larger animals.

"This is Bones, she's been here for six weeks," Hannah concluded the tour with one of their long-timers. The dog was a mixture of something fluffy and something spotty. It kind of made a weird looking Dalmatian.

"She's so cute," Veronica exclaimed, turning her attention to the dog and speaking baby. "Why hasn't someone adopted you? You're such a cute little puppy-wuppy." The dog just stared back at her like she was crazy. "Oh well, I tried. I see Harry the hottie is playing nice with Jessie the boyfriend stealer."

"Shh," Hannah whispered, grabbing her hand and dragging Veronica back to the kittens and away from the window. "They might hear you."

"I can't believe Harry is actually falling for her routine. I thought he was better than that."

"Let's not talk about it," Hannah replied, fearing she might start to cry if she confided everything she was feeling.

Veronica could see the pain in her eyes, she didn't need to say anything. "Is your shift over? How about we go get some ice cream, my shout?"

"How can I refuse?"

"You can't, come on," Veronica said decidedly. She linked her arm through Hannah's and led her out. Nothing cured a broken heart like ice cream.

Chapter 4

"There is nothing in my closet, it's official," Hannah said as she slumped down on her bed. She had searched twice already for something to wear to Harry's party and every time she came up empty.

"That's because you never go anywhere," Veronica declared. "Maybe if you let loose and got out more, you'd have nicer clothes."

Hannah shrugged, she was probably right. Veronica had lots of nice going out clothes in her wardrobe. She seriously needed a closet makeover. "What kind of outfit should I wear? I want Harry's parents to like me."

"Forget about his parents, you need something to knock Harry the hottie's socks off. You can make him forget all about Jessie."

"I definitely don't have anything that will do that," she sighed. She didn't even know if having a knockout outfit would be enough. Jessie was beautiful, confident, and from his neighborhood. She was everything Hannah wasn't and it only made her feel horrible every time she thought about it. "Maybe I shouldn't even go."

"Of course you are going," Veronica said sternly. "You will go and have a great time and by the end of the night it will be 'Jessie who?'."

"I think we need to go shopping," Coco's voice rang out from the doorway, startling them both. Neither girl had noticed her intrusion. "Who's up for it?"

Veronica looked at Hannah, waiting for her to eagerly agree. She didn't quite get the reaction she was hoping for. "I guess so."

Without any further ado, Coco grabbed her car keys and the girls huddled in the back of her VW Beetle, circa 1960. They chugged down the road, the exhaust only spluttering every few miles.

They ended up at the Mapleton Mall. It was a strip of shops that Hannah normally avoided. She wasn't a fashionista, quite the opposite. She normally dressed for comfort, if she looked good then it was a side bonus. Thankfully, Veronica and Coco were the exact opposite.

"How about this one?" Coco asked, holding up a dress covered in shimmering sequins. "It's pretty, right?"

Hannah vehemently shook her head. Over her dead body would she want to sparkle like that. "No way. I need something plain. It's a garden party, not a nightclub." Coco replaced the dress and kept flicking through the hangers.

Veronica found a navy blue short jumpsuit. "This

would look really cute on you, your legs would look amazing in the shorts."

One glance at the length and Hannah already felt naked just looking at it. "I want to be more covered." Veronica rolled her eyes and put it back. They continued that way for almost an hour. Everything they found had something wrong with it.

Growing more and more desperate, Hannah was starting to panic. The party was only a day away. If she didn't get anything now, then she wouldn't have anything to wear. There was no time to trawl the entire town for an outfit.

"I've got it," Veronica exclaimed. She held up a cotton pink dress with straps just thicker than spaghetti. It didn't look like there was enough material but Hannah was getting worried. The concern was evident as she grimaced. "Just try it on. It won't kill you to just try it."

"Fine," she sighed, taking the hanger. She trudged off to the change rooms, with her mother and best friend in tow. Hannah quickly changed, believing it was just a waste of time anyway. Pink wasn't her favorite colour and she liked to at least be able to bend over in an outfit without her panties showing.

With the dress finally on, Hannah stared at herself in the mirror. The outfit was simple, just a dress that went in at the waist and tied at the back with a belt made out of the same material. The sweetheart neckline was flattering but it was lower cut than anything she normally wore.

Taking a deep breath, she pulled back the curtain and awaited the reaction as they studied her.

It didn't take long. "You look so beautiful," Coco

gushed. "Just like a young woman."

"Seriously, Han, you look amazing," Veronica added. Hannah turned back to the mirror, trying to see what they did. To her, she just looked like an uncomfortable girl in a pink dress. She couldn't see the beauty or amazement they did.

"I don't know…"

"One look at you in that dress and Harry won't be able to take his eyes off you," Veronica continued, her own eyes wide open with awe.

"As long as that's all he keeps on you," Coco said, warningly. "I don't trust any teenage boy around you in that dress."

"It shows too much, doesn't it?" Hannah asked, looking at her figure. The only good thing about the dress would be that it was cool. She wouldn't swelter under the hot afternoon sun.

"It shows just enough. You have a cute little body, Hannah, I would have killed to look like that when I was your age. You should make the most of it while you have it."

Hannah ignored her mother and turned to Veronica, trusting her opinion more for things like fashion. "Do you really think I look nice?"

Veronica rolled her eyes, frustrated that she couldn't see it for herself. "It's a twelve on the scale of one to ten. Trust me, Han."

With one last look in the mirror, Hannah was resigned to the fact that this was her outfit. She just hoped Harry and his parents liked it as much as her cheer squad did.

Chapter 5

"Are you sure you want to wear that?" Coco asked, for the twentieth time since Hannah got dressed. "It looks a little... odd. If you're quick you can still take it off."

"I don't care, it makes me feel better," Hannah replied. She was wearing the pink dress but she had put a white singlet underneath it to cover what cleavage was showing. Layering was in, right? She was just getting into the swing of the fashion while ensuring her modesty was maintained.

Pulling up outside Harry's house and seeing it for the first time was enough to make her forget about her outfit. She had much bigger things to worry about. The house was huge, easily as big as four houses combined. The white fence that surrounded the entire structure was tall and imposing.

"Are you going to be okay?" Coco asked, seeing Hannah shrinking into her shell right before her eyes. "You can call me whenever you want to come home.

I'll drop whatever I'm doing and race right over."

Hannah took a deep breath, she knew she had to go in there. If she didn't, then she would lose Harry and that was the last thing she wanted. She needed to be brave, even though it was completely scary.

"I'll be okay," she finally replied, not convincing either of them. "Thank you for dropping me off."

"Remember I'm only a call away and these people are not better than you. Don't forget that they only have money, that doesn't make them special. It just means they can afford more stuff."

"Thanks, Mom," Hannah said, actually smiling for the first time since they left home. She left the safety of the car and headed towards the gates.

Inside, there were people everywhere, huddled together in little groups. Hannah felt like she stuck out, like every time someone looked at her they knew she didn't belong there. She desperately wished to find Harry.

She weaved her way around the ground floor of the house. Every wall held an expensive looking painting and every table boasted a valuable ornament. She worried about accidently knocking one off, they were probably worth more than a month of her mom's salary.

In her growing unease, Hannah considered leaving. She hadn't seen Harry which meant he hadn't seen her. She could slip out and pretend she was never there, overcome with the flu or something.

She turned to leave, deciding that flight was a better option than fight. She headed for the door, her hand grasped tight around her phone and ready to call. Her mother wouldn't have gotten too far away yet.

She almost made it out too before a hand gripped around her arm, stopping her mid-step. "Hannah, you made it!"

She spun around to face Harry, sighing with relief at seeing him. "Yeah, I just got here," she lied. "Everything looks great."

Harry shrugged. "It's all boring. But now you're here, that's definitely going to change. Come on, I'll show you around."

Without a choice, Hannah gripped onto Harry's hand tightly and allowed herself to be led through the people. She had already seen a lot of it already but didn't want to admit that. They stepped outside where more tables and people lingered underneath a large makeshift tent. The entire party looked like it could have been taken out of an entertaining magazine.

They stopped in front of a couple. "Hannah, I'd like you to meet my parents, Barry and Katrina Shephard. Mom, Dad, this is Hannah."

"It's nice to meet you," Hannah said quietly, trying to remember every manner her mother had taught her since she was born. She didn't want to put one foot out of place.

"It's a pleasure for us too," Katrina replied, smiling warmly. "Harry has told us so much about you. I feel like we already know you."

Hannah stole a glance at Harry, wondering what on Earth he had told them. She was too mortified to speak. Thankfully, she didn't have to.

"Anyone that keeps our son out of trouble," Barry added. "Is fine with us. You keep up the good work, Hannah." He winked.

Harry tugged at her hand. "We're going to go

dance. See you around."

They watched them leave. Hannah's brain started functioning again. The couple had seemed too young to have a son Harry's age. Perhaps her mother was right, rich people didn't get wrinkles because they didn't have to worry so much.

Harry didn't stop walking until they reached the nearly empty grassed area in front of the live band. A few brave couples were dancing to the music. He spun her around and moved into a dance position, his right arm around her waist and the other gripping her hand tightly at shoulder height.

Flashbacks to the only other time they had danced together kept repeating in Hannah's mind. The uncoordinated movements, the guy who spilt his entire drink on her white shirt, the panic. It wasn't a good movie reel to watch.

"So, you really live here?" Hannah asked, trying to distract herself. She was in Harry's arms, surely she couldn't go too wrong on the dance floor when he was leading her? She hoped not, although her own clumsiness never ceased to amaze her sometimes.

"Ever since I was born," Harry replied. "Do you like it? I know it's a bit… much."

"It's beautiful." Images of her own home in comparison popped into her head. What must Harry think about her tiny little house?

"My parents have to work day and night to pay for it all. I barely see them. It's why I started volunteering at the shelter, I wanted to actually have people around."

The confession took Hannah by surprise. She had assumed everything would have been perfect in

Harry's life. Didn't wealth buy you all the happiness you needed? She thought about Coco and how she saw her more than she wanted to. It gave her a whole new appreciation for not having everything.

"You have plenty of people around now," Hannah pointed out, thinking about her and Cory, plus Jessie of course. "I hope you're not lonely anymore."

Harry grinned. "Not when I have you." The familiar burn started in her cheeks. She looked away, fearing she might just completely break down with embarrassment if she didn't.

Suddenly the music changed, going from slow to fast. It was one of Hannah's favorite songs and definitely not what she had expected at a posh garden party. Harry let go of her hands, she stood there, not wanting to make a fool of herself.

"Come on, dance," Harry urged. He started pulling out the cheesiest dance moves imaginable. All the classics were there – the Sprinkler, the Lawnmower, the Saturday Night Fever jive, he even threw in Gangham Style. She couldn't help giggling as she joined in.

Nobody else was paying attention to them. Or, if they were, they didn't notice. They were too lost in the daggy dancing and having too much fun to feel self-conscious.

It was very rare that Hannah let herself have fun without having to think it through a thousand times first. Yet on the dance floor at the garden party, she didn't care about how she *should* act or what she *should* do. Harry had a way of making her forget about everything else and losing herself in the moment.

Chapter 6

They lost track of time dancing and only stopped when they ran out of energy. "Do you want a drink?" Harry asked, trying to regain his breath. Hannah just nodded and they left the tent for the house.

Food and freshly poured drinks were lined up on the back veranda, attended to by a dozen caterers. They filled a plate each and grabbed a champagne flute of orange juice. Harry led her back onto the lawn and through a set of trees.

The music was quieter back there and nobody else dared venture that far. They reached Harry's tree house and went inside. The little hut was only a foot off the ground.

Inside were traces of Harry's childhood – crayon drawings on the walls of suns and monsters, a stray matchbox car, and a single page of an X-Men comic. They sat on the floor, their dinner plate in front of them.

"This place is really cool," Hannah commented. "Did you used to play here all the time?"

"Only every single day."

"Veronica has a cubby house in her backyard. We used to play house all the time."

Harry mocked being offended. "This isn't a house, it's a fortress. Only the bravest of knights or cowboys or superheroes are allowed to enter."

Hannah giggled. "Which one am I?"

He didn't even need to think about it. "You're a superhero, Puppy Rescuer, defender of all those with hairy tails."

"Does that make you my plucky sidekick?" She asked, her eyes twinkling from laughter.

"I'll be your sidekick. Except, it's usually the sidekick that gets killed or kidnapped or something."

Hannah pursed her lips together in thought. "You could be Kitten Man, the finder of homes."

Harry stood on his knees, puffing his chest out while putting his hands on his hips. He spoke in an overly-deep voice. "I am Kitten Man, leader of the fluffy little cats."

"Has quite a ring to it."

He sat back down. "Maybe we'll keep working on it. How's your food?"

"Delicious. This whole party isn't exactly what I thought it would be," Hannah confessed, looking at her meal instead of at him.

"What were you expecting?"

"I don't know, I guess a lot of rich people that were kind of... snobby."

"A lot of them are," Harry replied honestly. "But my parents aren't like that. They had nothing when they got married. They earned every single dollar they made by hard work. They're kind of my heroes."

Hannah's eyes shot up to meet his. "They used to be poor?"

He nodded. "My parents grew up with nothing, they don't take anything for granted. They never let me get too spoilt because they don't want me growing up feeling like the world owes me."

It was a revelation to Hannah, she just assumed Harry's family were always rich. She never imagined they had once been just like her mother. She suddenly understood why Harry was so unaffected, his parents had succeeded in keeping him grounded.

"So it doesn't bother you that my family don't have much then?" Hannah asked, it was a question she had asked herself many times before.

"Of course it doesn't. I'm with you because you're you. Not because of what you own." His words brought a smile to her lips. Apparently she had been the only one stressing about who had what. She felt silly for making such a big deal out of it. Thankfully Harry didn't know all that went on inside her head.

Harry broke the silence before it settled in for good. "If you're finished with dinner, I want to show you something."

Hannah placed the knife and fork neatly onto the plate. "All ready."

He grinned, taking her hand in his as they stood. He turned right, leading her further away from the party. They walked down a track of stones to a pond. It wasn't just a little backyard pond with a few koi fish bumping into each other, it was more of a small lake. Large boulders surrounded the banks, along with a smattering of palms, ferns, and other plants.

The sun had disappeared behind the horizon, leaving the moon and stars to fill the sky. Harry picked up a small pebble from the path. "Watch this." He threw the stone into the pond, sending it skimming across the top. Each time it hit the water, a burst of light rippled out from the impact.

"Phosphorescence," Hannah gasped. The naturally occurring light display was so beautiful, like their own set of fireworks in the pond.

"My dad's kind of a nerd when it comes to things like that," Harry explained. "He says it reminds him of when he was a kid and went fishing with his dad."

Hannah picked up a pebble and threw it into the water. It only skipped twice but the lights that lit up upon impact were just as beautiful. "It's amazing."

"You're amazing."

She stopped, still holding the next pebble in her hand. Everything was so perfect she didn't understand what she had done to deserve it.

Suddenly, she couldn't think anymore. Harry wrapped her in his arms, pulling her close. Their lips found each other in the moonlight. Hannah relaxed into him, dropping the pebble so she could place her hands on his chest. He cradled her cheeks, the warmth burning in the best way possible.

When he let her go, she giggled. She didn't mean to and it probably wasn't appropriate, but she couldn't stop herself. The whole party was so unexpectedly enjoyable that the burst of happiness couldn't be suppressed.

"I'm glad my kissing technique is so funny," Harry said teasingly. "I'm so happy you find my attempts hilarious."

She found it difficult to catch her breath, no matter how much she wanted to explain herself. "Your kissing technique is perfect. I'm just happy. These kinds of things don't happen to me, they happen to other girls. Not me."

"Not if I have anything to do with it."

She finally stopped laughing, looking into Harry's eyes and seeing only a look of love there. She took a step back, embarrassed all of a sudden at being so close to him. She turned her eyes skywards, looking at the millions of stars twinkling back at them.

"See that star there?" She said, pointing to a particularly bright one. She remembered back to when Harry had done the same thing on the beach. She wondered if he remembered it too.

He joined her, snaking his arm around her back. She leant her head on his shoulder, thinking how perfectly it fit there. "I see the star."

"It's called Corioses and it was discovered in 1932. Can you believe it's been burning so bright for all that time?" Hannah remembered when her father had told her about that particular star. She couldn't believe it was older than her grandmother.

"That's a long time," Harry agreed. He pointed to another star. "Tell me about that one."

Hannah took a deep breath before launching into the story behind the next star. She lost track of how long they were standing there in the moonlight discussing the stars. All she knew was that when Coco picked her up, she was in her pajamas.

Chapter 7

Nothing was going to dampen Hannah's mood. Not when she had an idea for saving the animals. She hurried into the shelter, desperate to tell everyone.

"Cory, I know how we can raise the money," she started eagerly. Harry joined them at the office door, making sure he didn't miss out on what was exciting her so much. "All we have to do-"

"You are never going to guess who my dad got for the concert," Jessie interrupted, parading into the shelter like she owned the place.

"Who? Don't keep us guessing," Cory insisted.

"Yeah, we want to know," Harry added. Hannah remained quiet, her idea overshadowed by the news.

"Lady Antelope," Jessie said, beaming with pride. "They've agreed to perform and we'll have them for the entire day. How great is it going to be?"

Cory squealed. "I love them!"

"I know, right? They're like the best."

"Well done, Jess," Harry commended, patting her on the back. He turned to Hannah. "It's great news, huh?"

Hannah forced a smile to her lips. "Great, really great." She didn't want to join in the celebrations. Instead, she picked up a broom and got to work while they raved on about how wonderful the concert was going to be.

She knew she should be happy that Jessie's dad booked Lady Antelope for the concert. They were a big deal, she knew they would have no problems selling tickets with them on board. But she couldn't stop the feelings of jealousy that engulfed her. They had wasted no time in dismissing her for Princess Jessie. That was the fact that hurt the most.

She spent the rest of the morning avoiding everyone. Harry, Cory, and Jessie were all walking on clouds with the news. Their smiles and laughter just grated on Hannah's nerves. Every sweep of the broom or swipe of the cloth grew more and more forceful. If she didn't get out of there soon, she was going to explode.

"Hey, Hannah," Harry called out, getting her attention. "Do you feel like helping me hang posters for the concert?"

It was the outing she desperately needed. "Sure," she replied, putting down the mop she was holding. She placed a *Slippery When Wet* sign on the floor and hurried out.

Harry was waiting on his bicycle, a stack of freshly printed posters underneath his arm. "I thought we'd cover the town in concert ads. What do you think?"

"You only have concert posters there?" He nodded

in response. "Wait here while I grab something."

She raced inside and grabbed a pile of kitten posters. If they were going to blanket the city, she wanted to make sure everyone knew they had kittens for adoption too. Even if one failed, hopefully the other wouldn't.

She hurried back outside and tied the posters to the back of the bike. It would be a bit of a juggling act but she would do it. They set off and headed for anywhere they could hang posters – notice boards, light poles, parking garages, anywhere there was a blank canvas. And even some not so blank places got a cover too.

Next to each of the concert posters, Hannah made sure to hang *Kittens For Adoption* signs too. If the headline act didn't get their attention, then a cute fluffy kitten would. Hannah knew which one would get her eyes to look first and it wasn't the concert.

As they started cycling back after all the posters were gone, Harry slowed down so they could talk. "The concert's going to be amazing. We'll have that twenty thousand easy."

"We'd better," Hannah replied. She didn't mean it to sound as curt as it actually did.

"What do you mean?"

"I guess I'm just nervous that we're putting all our hopes on one concert," she tried to explain, feeling like she was just wasting her breath. "If something happens, then we don't have a backup plan. The shelter will close."

Harry shook his head. "How could it not work? It's Lady Antelope. Those kinds of bands never play in places like this. Everyone in town will go to it, perhaps even some from around the place. They'll travel just to see them."

Hannah shrugged, her theory of wasting her breath confirmed. There was no point in arguing, it was Princess Jessie that could do no wrong. "I hope you're right."

"Of course we're right. We're going to save the shelter." He smiled, trying to reassure her. She couldn't believe she was the only one that was seeing sense in the whole plan. Putting all your eggs in one basket was risky and, considering the lives of dozens of animals was at stake, she didn't think the potential reward outweighed the risk. Her scientific brain wouldn't allow it.

They returned to the shelter in silence. The outing helped Hannah calm down a bit from her frustration but only slightly. She started feeding the dogs, hoping they would bring a smile to her face. Harry followed close behind.

"You don't agree with the concert, do you?" He asked, finally getting it.

Hannah stopped, mid-scoop, to look at him. "I'm worried about the animals. At the end of the day, we can go home to our houses and pretend like everything is okay. These animals can't. We are all they have and if they don't have the shelter, then they won't have a future. I want to protect them."

He took a step to stand beside her, placing his hands on her shoulder, he give her a squeeze. "It's going to be okay. The concert will keep the doors open, you'll see. The animals will all be fine. We wouldn't let anything happen to this place, you know that."

She didn't know that, not for sure and she knew he

didn't either. His gentle lies were not enough, not when the stakes were so high. "But what happens if we fail? What happens if we have to shut the doors?"

"We won't let it get to that point."

"So we'll just magically conjure up the twenty thousand dollars we need?" She shrugged his hands away, not wanting to be near him suddenly. The room felt too small and stuffy. She placed the food bowl in the dog's cage to cover her discomfort.

"We'll get it someway. My parents-" He was cut off as Jessie entered, interrupting was starting to become a habit.

"Oh, good, Harry you're back. I can't remember how to mix the rabbit food. Will you show me?" She cocked her head to one side, just like the dogs did when they were silently asking a question.

Hannah wasn't going to let Harry fall for her ruse. She could see right through the girl. She stepped forward. "I'll show you. Harry can finish feeding the dogs."

The disappointment was written across her face. "Oh, if you're sure, that would be great. Thanks." Jessie disappeared back through the doorway. Hannah followed, not even looking for Harry's reaction.

She mixed the food, giving clear instructions as she went. It wasn't like it was hard – one scoop of grain to every scoop of the mixture. One for one, it wasn't rocket science. Maybe just for Jessie it was hard, Hannah thought.

After they fed the rabbits, Hannah had an idea. Coco's voice was replaying in her mind, telling her to befriend the girl instead of thinking of her as an enemy. "Hey, Jessie, do you want me to help you bathe the dogs? That was on your list today, right?"

"Yeah, that would be great," Jessie replied eagerly. Together, they ran the water and pulled the first dog from the cages. Hannah made sure it was the little white one, the one that loved jumping out of the bath when you were least expecting it.

"We should start with Toto," she said, slowly placing the dog into the warm water.

Hannah stood back and just watched it unfold. She only felt slightly guilty as Jessie was soon splashed and covered in water. So much for her expensive, dry clean only outfit. She should have known better than to wear it to an animal shelter.

She giggled, trying not to laugh. "I guess he's not enjoying the bath so much."

"You think?" Jessie grumbled, trying to get a hold of the sopping wet dog.

Hannah couldn't take it anymore, the whole scene was way too funny. Finally, Jessie was getting some of the true shelter experience – just like everyone else who had volunteered there. "Do you need help?"

Jessie *humphed*, trying to blow back the stray pieces of hair over her face while her hands were occupied. Hannah stepped in, not wanting the dog to suffer from her incompetence. She pulled Toto from the water and held a towel up while he shook himself.

"Did you enjoy that boy, huh?" She cooed, like she didn't have a problem in the world. She towel dried the dog as best she could while Jessie cleaned herself up. Not that there was much she could do, she didn't exactly bring a change of clothes with her.

"Maybe you should grab Ruffles before you dry, he's a bit of a jumper too," Hannah suggested, nodding towards one of the other cages where a fat Labrador lay down. Jessie groaned and followed her directions.

The next two hours was spent the same way. By the end of it, there was not one part of Jessie still dry. From head to foot, she was covered in dog bath water and soapy suds. Her outfit, along with her perfectly done hair, were almost unrecognizable.

Guilt started to creep onto Hannah's radar. She didn't normally enjoy seeing people suffer, but it wasn't anything she hadn't gone through herself when she first started volunteering. It was a ritual, all the newbie's got to bath the animals. She was just lucky she hadn't told her to bath the cats instead. *That* was a painful experience.

"What should I do now?" Jessie finally asked, using one of the dog's towels to dry her hair. Hannah was mildly surprised, she expected her to run home even though her shift wasn't finished yet.

Hannah looked around, trying to work out what else needed to be done. There was one thing, but was she cruel enough to get her to do it? *Would* she do it?

"Uh, the cages need cleaning?" She half asked, half suggested.

"All the cages?"

"We have to do them regularly or the animals might get sick. Plus, it makes everything smell much better in here."

Jessie sighed. "Where do I start?"

Hannah reached over and grabbed a dustpan, handing it over. "Start with the big stuff first and then disinfect."

She watched as Jessie got to work. Hannah

retreated to the kittens, making sure the mothers and babies were okay. As she saw Jessie struggling with the mess, she started to wonder whether she had misjudged her.

Sure, Jessie was a spoilt little rich girl and she was probably manipulating Harry to spend time with him. If Hannah turned her back and let her guard down, she would probably stab her in the back too. But Jessie was trying. She could have given up and she definitely didn't have to follow Hannah's directions.

But she did and she was actually doing it pretty well. And without complaining. A pang of guilt was definitely creeping in.

Chapter 8

"Thanks for riding home with me," Hannah said with a smile as she walked her bike up the driveway.

"It was my pleasure," Harry replied, dismounting too as he joined her. "I kind of feel bad for not spending more time with you lately."

Hannah stopped, crinkling her nose as she wondered what he meant. "We see each other at the shelter nearly every day."

He shrugged, it was adorable. "I know but I've been teaching Jessie a fair bit. It takes time away from you and the kittens."

"In that case, the kittens miss you. They told me so." She grinned, teasing. "Do you think Jessie will stick around for the rest of the summer?"

"I think so," Harry replied, glancing away for just a moment as he considered what to say. "She's got some trouble at home, her parents are divorcing. They're arguing about everything, it's just a mess. She doesn't want to be there at the moment."

The afternoon's events flashed through Hannah's mind. Now she knew she felt guilty. "I didn't know, I'm sorry for her. It can't be easy." She remembered when her parents had divorced. Even though they both told her it wasn't her fault, she still felt like it was. She just wanted it to be a bad dream that she would wake up from and everything would be fine. "Is her dad moving out? That's what mine did. He moved away and I barely see him anymore."

Harry nodded sadly. "He is. She's taking it pretty bad, that's why I suggested she join us at the shelter."

"You're a good friend," Hannah replied sincerely. All that time and she had just assumed Jessie was trying to steal her boyfriend when she was really just trying to escape a stressful home situation. She didn't normally misjudge people but she knew she had now.

Harry leaned over and gave her a quick hug before hopping back on his bicycle. "I'll see you tomorrow."

"See you." Hannah waved while he disappeared down the street. She went inside, hoping she wasn't as mean to Jessie as she felt like she was.

Billy greeted her at the door, his tail wagging like it was about to fall off. She crouched down and gave him a cuddle. "Hey boy, you want to play outside?"

At hearing the magic words, the dog took off into the backyard. Hannah followed, not quite as enthusiastic. She threw a ball for Billy, giggling as he chased it and refused to return it to her. He always liked hogging the ball, she would have to chase him for it if she wanted to throw it again.

As she ran around the backyard, at least one of the burdens she had been carrying was lifted. Jessie didn't want Harry, she wanted to get out of her house. Perhaps they were going to be okay after all.

She felt lighter for the rest of the night, even though a little guilty. When it came time to return to the shelter the next day, she was back to her happy self again. The previous day was just a single day in her life, she didn't have to dwell on it.

Harry's bike was already leaning against the wall when she arrived. She parked hers next to it and went inside, wondering what the day would bring. She hoped it would be quieter than usual so she could spend some extra time with the animals. With all the stress and worry of the fundraising, she thought for sure they could sense that something bad was going on.

As she stepped through, all was quiet as hoped. She checked in with Cory in her office.

"Good morning, Cory, how's it going?" Hannah asked, trying to keep the mood upbeat. Her boss was standing at her desk, filling a box with files. "What are you doing?"

"Just packing a few things." She smiled, not stopping what she was doing.

"Why? We aren't going anywhere."

"I have to prepare for the worst case scenario," Cory explained sadly. "If we don't raise the money, then we're going to have to leave pretty quickly. I'll be busy with the animals, I don't want to have to worry about getting the paperwork in order."

"Do you really think it's going to come to that?" Hannah panicked, if Cory didn't believe they could do it, then they were stuffed. She was the only adult among them, perhaps they were all fooling themselves that they could do it.

"I hope not," she sighed. "But I do have to be prepared. Hopefully I'll be unpacking these boxes in a week's time."

"What will happen to the animals?" Hannah asked. She had already asked Harry but knew he wouldn't tell her the truth. She had a horrible feeling in the pit of her stomach about the fate of the animals and she prayed she was wrong.

Cory stopped and looked at her. For just a moment, Hannah thought she might burst into tears before she regained her composure. "I'll personally try to re-house them into another shelter. These furry, four legged things are my life. You have my promise that I won't let anything happen to them. I'll take them all home with me if I have to."

"I'll take half," Hannah grinned. She would too. Explaining it to Coco would be another matter, but she would deal with the consequences. Her mother would understand.

They were interrupted as a laughing Harry and Jessie joined them, fresh from an early morning walk with the dogs. Harry gave Hannah a quick squeeze of the arm in greeting.

"You're in a good mood this morning," Hannah commented, wondering what was so funny. Considering their dire situation, it didn't seem appropriate to be so overwhelmingly happy.

Jessie answered for both of them. "We sold half the tickets last night."

"You did?!" Cory and Hannah said in unison with the same shocked tone.

Harry nodded proudly. "My neighbor was having a

party so we crashed it and sold every person there a ticket. When we said Lady Antelope was performing, they went nuts."

"We're totally going to save the shelter," Jessie added. They exchanged a glance, it was a little too familiar for Hannah's liking.

"Well done guys. But that still leaves a lot of tickets. We can't get too excited yet, we have a long way to go," Cory said, the voice of reason. "We can't afford to think we've already done it." They nodded somberly. "And we've got poop to scoop, so back to work." She added a smile to the order.

Hannah put her bag down and started getting to work. She volunteered for kitten duty. Cleaning their cages was a tricky feat with the little scamps insisting on helping, but it also allowed for lots of cuteness.

As she worked, she thought about the concert. With her new knowledge of Jessie, she saw it all in a different light. Perhaps the concert was a good idea after all. If they managed to sell half the tickets in just one night, imagine how easy it would be to sell the rest in one week.

It was a really great thing getting her dad to book Lady Antelope. Jessie didn't have to help that much but she had, even when things at home were a mess. They were actually going to pull it off, the thought lifted her spirits like nothing else. They would raise the money for the shelter and keep the doors open for at least another year.

Who knows? Maybe the concert could be an annual event? If Jessie's dad had that many connections, he might be able to get someone just as good for the next concert. They might even be able to make more money once the concerts become well known. People would come from all over to attend every year.

After her shift ended, Hannah met with Veronica. Their sole mission was to sell as many concert tickets as possible. It was less than a week until the big day, they needed to move as many as they could.

They decided their best bet was to go door to door with the tickets. It would take them until nightfall, but people would find it more difficult to say no if they were being asked one on one. That was Hannah's theory, anyway. She was curious to see if she was right.

They walked up and down the streets together, one house after the next. Their strike rate was about fifty-fifty. Their ticket supply was dwindling, just not as fast as they had hoped.

"At least we're selling some," Hannah commented, not wanting Veronica to give up just yet.

"My feet are killing me," she moaned.

"You knew you were going walking, why did you wear high heels?" Hannah giggled. It was so Veronica to put fashion over functionality.

"Because they make my calves look fabulous," Veronica replied, shrugging it off. "Speaking of things that look fabulous, are you and Harry going to come to the bonfire on the beach party?"

In everything else that had been going on, Hannah had completely forgotten about the annual event. It was a celebration of summer, every teenager in Mapleton attended. "I think I might skip it."

"But I've already told Lucas you're coming. He likes hanging out with Harry, he thinks he's funny."

"I'm sorry," Hannah apologized, feeling that now familiar feeling of guilt creep in again. "I just don't really feel like partying when the shelter could be closing."

Veronica waved the ticket book around. "It's not closing, we're selling these babies. It's going to stay open. So now you don't have an excuse not to come." She watched Hannah closely, examining every inch of her face. "Unless there's another reason why you don't want to come?"

"Like what?" She asked, hoping Veronica wouldn't get to the truth. There were only a few things she kept from her best friend and this was one of them. Right now, she didn't want to get into her problems with Harry and how she was still overcome with doubts about the whole relationship. Even knowing more about Jessie couldn't put all her fears at bay. There was something else wrong and she couldn't quite put her finger on it. Until she could, she would keep it to herself.

"I don't know," Veronica admitted. "But you know I'm here to talk to, right? Will you just think about the party at least? I'd like you to be there."

"I'll think about it."

Satisfied, Veronica linked her arm through Hannah's and they approached the next house. She hoped it held an army of people, enough to get rid of the rest of the tickets so she could quit walking.

Chapter 9

The day before the concert, Hannah was feeling pretty confident about the whole thing. With all but a few of the tickets sold, everyone at the shelter was. The money raised from the tickets alone was almost at their goal. A bit more on the day and they would be able to definitively say they could keep the doors open for another year.

Checking on the kittens after she fed them, Hannah heard a noise that sounded like someone was having a stern conversation. The problem was, it sounded like they were having it with themselves.

She followed the noise, looking around to see if anyone else heard it. Harry and Cory were both busy with people in reception. She continued on, all the way to Cory's office. Hannah opened the door quietly, seeing Jessie in the room alone.

"Are you okay?" She asked.

When Jessie turned to face her, her eyes were bright

red and wet from crying. She just shook her head in response. Hannah hurried in, closing the door behind her, and gave her a hug.

"What's wrong? Has something happened with your parents?" Hannah asked, hoping she wasn't getting Harry in trouble for mentioning it.

She wiped her eyes, trying to calm down. "It's nothing, really. Just parent stuff I guess. I'll be fine."

It wasn't like they were BFF's so Hannah didn't feel right prying any more than she already had. Hysterical people made her uncomfortable, she never knew what to do or say. Veronica had done it to her on several occasions. She would normally just pat her back and hope that helped in some way.

"Are you sure?" Hannah asked instead. Jessie nodded, faking a smile in response. "Okay, well tell me if you need anything."

She left her alone in the office to calm down, figuring she probably didn't need an audience for her meltdown. She closed the door again. However, as she did, Jessie started talking to herself again.

She pressed her ear up against the door, hoping nobody would catch her eavesdropping. It wasn't normally something she condoned herself but Jessie was so upset, she was worried about her.

The words came through muffled but there was no denying them. "You are so stupid, Jessie. Everybody is going to show up tomorrow expecting Lady Antelope and they're not going to be there. They're all going to know what a big liar you are."

Hannah gasped, covering her mouth to stop herself. She kept listening, hoping she was mistaken.

"My daddy has booked Lady Antelope, why did I

have to say that? Seriously, what's wrong with me? Everyone's going to hate me. Stupid, Jessie, stupid."

She stepped away from the door as Jessie's footsteps stomped around the office. Hannah reeled, her mind racing with everything. If Jessie had made up Lady Antelope being booked for the concert, then they had no concert. No concert meant no money. They would have to refund all the ticket sales and call the whole thing off. They didn't have time for another fundraiser.

Hannah stumbled into the dog's area. Looking around at all the sad faces, their futures were completely bleak now. She would definitely have to make good on her promise, Cory would take half and she would house the other half. It was going to be their only option.

Or would it? There was no way she could let the shelter close. She had to do something to fix everything, even if it wasn't her fault that they were in that mess. Perhaps there was something she could do to salvage everything. If Jessie wasn't going to come clean about it, then nobody else would be doing anything. And Hannah could not let that happen.

She raced past reception, grabbing her handbag as she went. "Cory, I have to go. I'm sorry, I'll see you tomorrow."

"It's the concert tomorrow, don't forget," she called back.

Hannah almost smiled, how could she forget? The fate of the whole thing rested on her shoulders now. She jumped on her bicycle, dialing her phone as she did. There was only one person who could help her and she just prayed Veronica would be answering.

"Hey, Han, what's up?" Veronica's happy voice finally came on the line.

"I need your help."

"What can I do?"

Hannah knew exactly what she could do. "Meet me at my house as soon as you can? We need to save the fundraiser."

"Give me ten," Veronica replied before hanging up.

Hannah peddled as fast as she could. With less than twenty-four hours until the concert was supposed to start, she had her work cut out for her.

Chapter 10

Adrenalin, fear, hope, and coffee coursed through Hannah's veins as she walked into Beresford Park. She flashed her volunteer lanyard at the ticket collector, praying she wouldn't be lynched once inside the doors. There were thousands of people waiting to see Lady Antelope perform, who knew what they would do when they didn't turn up.

She had barely slept a wink, spending all night trying to salvage what she could. She had no idea if it would work but it was the only way to save the shelter. More than anything else, she just wanted the animals to be safe. Whatever it took, right?

The backstage area was a hive of activity with Cory, Harry, and Jessie standing in amongst it all. People carried lights and sound machines around, setting them up where needed. Others spoke into walkie talkies, looking important. Hannah wasn't sure what they were actually doing. She joined the others, Harry giving her a smile hello.

"Did your father say when Lady Antelope would get here?" Cory asked, glancing at her watch. "They did know it was ten a.m., right? Not ten p.m.?

Jessie was looking decidedly ill. If Hannah had barely slept, she doubted whether Jessie had slept at all. "I, uh, don't know."

A din was filtering through from the waiting crowd on the other side of the makeshift stage. They were getting louder as the anticipation built and patience fell.

"I could go out there and stall for a bit," Harry offered. Cory shrugged desperately, quickly running out of options. Hannah checked her watch, her eyes flicking to the door every few seconds.

"You might need to," Cory sighed, turning to Jessie. "Could your dad maybe call them and check where they are? We don't want to be pushy, of course, but we kind of need to know what's going on."

Jessie swallowed, scratching her arm distractedly. She finally looked up. "Cory, there's something I need to tell you."

At that moment, Hannah saw movement at the door. Veronica peeked in, giving a thumbs up. It was the signal she had been waiting for. "Cory, Jessie just wants to tell you there has been a change of plans. But don't worry because everything is fine."

"What's going-" Cory never got to finish her sentence. With a wave of the hand, Veronica opened the black curtain separating them. She held it open as a stream of their friends marched in. One by one, the otherwise studious and quiet teenagers flowed in. The others just stared as Hannah took the lead.

"Guys, you can set up the stage and we'll get moving as soon as you're ready."

Jessie stared, glancing momentarily at Harry. "What's the nerd brigade got to do with this?" He just shrugged in response.

The next wave of teenagers brought with them an accessory – dogs, cats, rabbits, and a goat. They led the animals in, holding them close with their leashes. They formed a group on the other side of the backstage area, waiting patiently for their cue.

"Are those the animals from the shelter?" Cory gasped. "What are they doing here?"

"Saving the shelter," Hannah replied simply. She didn't have time to get into the details, not when the third wave of volunteers were just arriving.

The next group were the complete opposite of Hannah's friends. They mostly wore black skinny jeans and ironic old band t-shirts. They carried with them guitars, drum kits, microphones, and anything else they needed to perform. They moved to the front, waiting for instructions.

Hannah gathered them all together. "Thanks for coming guys. We'll get started in a minute."

Cory stopped Hannah mid-stride. "Hannah, what is going on? What are all these people doing here? And where is Lady Antelope?"

"They couldn't make it, they had a scheduling conflict," she answered quickly, looking over her shoulder at a wide eyed Jessie. "These guys are all going to make sure the people out there don't even miss Lady Antelope. I have to go. Don't worry, everything will be fine."

In a stunned silence, she let Hannah go. Everyone

was just staring at her in gaping surprise, Harry included. She pulled back the curtain and stepped on stage for the first time. Her legs were like jelly as she kept going, all the way until she reached the microphone standing like a lone soldier at the front.

She had never seen that many people before and that many people had definitely never been staring at her before. It was terrifying standing there, every one of them waiting on tenterhooks to hear what she had to say. Hannah knew at that moment that veterinary was definitely her career choice, not being a pop singer.

"Thanks for coming," Hannah said meekly, swallowing to try to get some moisture in her mouth. She looked down at the sea of faces, seeing individual people for the first time. Some she recognized, most she didn't. But what she saw next warmed her heart.

When Veronica, Coco, and herself had started a serious call around the previous afternoon, she had asked anyone coming to the concert to bring their pet. It wasn't just going to be a concert, but a celebration of animals. She didn't think people would actually listen to her. Yet on the ground, hairy faces were upturned towards her too. Dogs of all kinds were standing diligently with their human friends, their hairy tails wagging happily.

Hannah suddenly felt a calmness wash over her. She was going to do it, she was going to pull the whole thing off. She took a deep breath. "Thank you for coming. I know you were all expecting Lady Antelope and I'm sorry to say they have had to pull out at the last minute. What we have for you, however, is something much better. Today, for your entertainment, we have a battle of the bands. Please support these emerging superstars of tomorrow."

Silence. She looked around, half-expecting a riot to break out. People shuffled from foot to foot while they waited but there was no mass hysteria. She continued.

"So, without further ado, let's hear it for the first band. We have the Streakers from Mapleton High School." She stepped back and the band of four teenagers ran out on the stage. She held her breath.

As they picked up their instruments and strummed their first chord, the crowd erupted into a round of applause. Hannah couldn't remove the smile from her face as she retreated backstage again.

Chapter 11

Hannah couldn't believe how well the day had gone so far. It was just after lunchtime and they hadn't even got to her favorite part yet.

While the bands were great, and such good sports for turning up with such little notice, she had something extra special in store for everyone. They just didn't know it yet.

Cory approached, standing next to Hannah as she watched the crowds. She wasn't that interested in the bands, it was more fun to watch the pets in the audience as they talked to each other and enjoyed time with their humans.

"The bands are great, huh?" Cory commented, nudging her with her shoulder.

"Yeah, I think everyone loves them."

Silence lingered between them, although it wasn't awkward with so much to look at. Hannah sensed Cory wanted to say something, she waited patiently for what was about to come. Would she get in trouble for changing the schedule without telling her? Maybe she didn't want the animals to leave the shelter? She could only imagine what she was about to say.

"Hannah, I-"

"Before you say anything," Hannah butted in. "I'm sorry I took the animals out of the shelter. But there is something coming up that I needed them for."

Cory laughed. "I think what you've done is great. What I was going to say was that I don't really know what happened here this morning, but I wanted to thank you for it. Without you, none of this would have been possible, I'm sure." She gestured around to the stage and the audience. Not to mention the students playing with the shelter animals on the lawn.

"I really wanted to save the animals," Hannah confessed. That was the crux of it, anything else paled into comparison.

"Hopefully we'll do that. We've still got a way to go yet, but we're close."

Cory patted her on the shoulder before leaving her alone. Despite the joy at seeing the concert being successful, Hannah had thought it would be enough to save the shelter. She imagined the ticket sales would be sufficient. She was going to have to work even harder before the day was out.

"Hey," Harry said, sidling up to her. "This is amazing. So what really happened to Lady Antelope?"

Hannah stared at him, she had a lot to say to Harry but it would have to wait. It was a long story that she didn't want to get into. Not when the main show was just about to start.

"I have to go, Harry. I'll talk to you later." She

didn't look at him before hurrying over to her friends. "Five minutes to the show. Stylists, do your magic."

Hannah watched as a team of professional dog dressers from Pooch Couture, the fancy animal clothes boutique in town, gathered around the shelter animals. They had a designer outfit for each of them, pampering them like they had never experienced before.

By the time the clock struck one, every single animal looked like a million dollars. There were bows in hairs, a pug was dressed as a security officer, a poodle was parading around like a princess, the fluffy white dog that hated bathing was dressed in a yellow raincoat. Every animal was dressed to match their personality. Their coats had never looked shinier, their eyes never so alert, and their tails never so waggy.

Hannah lined them up and waited for the band to finish their set. She wasn't afraid of going on stage and talking to thousands of people this time, she was determined to raise enough money to keep the doors open. A bit of shyness was nothing compared with the tragedy of still having to close down the shelter.

The band left and took a bow to a deafening round of applause and cheer from the audience. They were pumped, it was an excellent way to lead into the main event.

She hurried out to the microphone and looked around. "Ladies and gentlemen, I hope you're enjoying the concert so far." She had to stop until the cheering subsided. "Excellent. Now, we have something special for you. I would like to introduce you to the animals from the shelter, wearing designer outfits from Pooch Couture who have been kind enough to donate their time and allow us to use their clothes."

Hannah nodded to her waiting friends backstage and they started streaming out. She couldn't be prouder of them for working so hard and offering to help without any notice. They were all the shy, quiet types too. Parading on stage was not something they would normally want to have done. Yet for the animals, they would all do anything.

"While you're welcoming them, please also give a round of applause to the Mapleton Student's Science Club for accompanying them on stage."

Smiles beamed at her, both from the animals and humans, as they passed by. They paraded around slowly.

"First we have a miniature fox terrier wearing a beautiful spotted outfit to match his own spots," Hannah started, praying her plan would work. "Maximus is available for adoption, along with all the animals you see here today. He's got a loving little spirit, always up for a game and, of course, a treat or two. He loves his food but he will love you even more. Let's give it up for Maximus."

The audience applauded, they were actually listening to her. And they were enjoying the show. If just one person in the audience fell in love with each of the animals, they would find a home for them. It only took one person to adopt.

Hannah went through each of the animals in turn, even showing off some grumpy looking cats in Halloween outfits. She just knew they were going to scratch her for the humiliation later on. Cats were like that, they remembered everything.

As they did their last loop around the stage,

Hannah couldn't believe how wonderful they all were. None of the pets looked like they had come from a shelter. They looked like loved and well cared for animals. She hoped with all her heart they would find a family to love them by the end of the day. Each and every one of them deserved it.

"If you would like to adopt any of these wonderful little creatures, please see me at the stand near the refreshments van. I'll be there all afternoon and it will be the best decision you've ever made. I adopted a rescue animal a few weeks ago and I can't tell you how much love he has brought into our home. A house isn't a home until you have a pet. Thank you."

She hurried off stage and crossed her fingers. Backstage was chaotic as the animals were removed from their clothes. Loose fur flew everywhere as the excited dogs jumped around and wanted to play some more.

Hannah thanked everyone profusely for their help before braving the throng of people and weaving her way through to the booth by the drinks stand.

She expected to have a quiet afternoon as the bands entertained the crowds. Perhaps a few people might adopt a dog here and there to break up the time.

What Hannah didn't expect to see was a queue of people waiting for her when she arrived. There were more people wanting to adopt than she had animals for.

By the end of the afternoon, she had a list of families just waiting to adopt. The moment they got something suitable into the shelter, they had first dibs.

And they didn't just want dogs. According to Hannah's tally, every single kitten in the shelter would find a new home the moment they returned to the office. Some people were even happy to take the mother cats too, preferring a more mature option than a bouncing kitten that was full of energy.

As the concert came to a close, Hannah was grateful everything had been salvaged from the train wreck it was heading into. There wasn't one person that left unhappy and not one animal that would return to the shelter – even the goat. She just hoped it would be enough to keep the doors open.

Chapter 12

Hannah was clearing up litter in the park, trying to restore the lawn to how it was before the concert. She was happy to see her friends helping alongside her. All the guests had left and the last of the bands were packing up their gear. That only left the clean up.

Jessie approached. Hannah hadn't seen her nearly all day. The last she knew, she was helping out with the ticket booth. "Hey, Hannah, can I have a word?"

"Sure," she replied, figuring her back could do with a break from bending over and picking up rubbish. "What's up?"

Jessie shuffled from foot to foot, clearly wanting to say something but unable to start. Hannah waited patiently, despite how eager she was to get the job over and done with.

Finally, the girl continued. "I, uh, just wanted to thank you for everything you did today. You could have let it be a complete disaster but you didn't. You didn't even tell Cory and Harry what I did."

Hannah actually felt sorry for her standing there. "You shouldn't have lied, but I don't need to tell you that. I just wanted to make sure the shelter stayed open, that's it."

Tears started to well in Jessie's eyes, she was coming apart right in front of her. "I just wanted everyone to like me. I thought if I said Lady Antelope would be here, then everyone would want me around even though I am absolutely hopeless at the shelter." The words poured from her mouth, interrupted by sobs.

Hannah put her arms around the girl and gave a hug. "We like you anyway. You didn't need to pretend to be something you're not. We would have found a way without the concert."

Jessie nodded as she let her go. "You really like me?"

"You're getting better at washing the dogs," Hannah teased, hoping to stop the tears. "A few more dozen and you should be right."

They laughed together. "Thanks, Hannah. You're a really good friend."

Hannah smiled, hoping they really could be friends. The shelter could use as many hands as possible and she didn't want to scare anyone off.

"Can I have your attention?" They were interrupted by Cory, standing on what was left of the stage. The microphone had been packed away, leaving the volunteers no option except to move closer to hear. "I have done a final count of the proceeds from today and our efforts right up until now."

Hannah had never been so anxious to hear the

news, and she had spent fifteen years awaiting exam results. She crossed both her fingers and toes, praying for the words she desperately wanted to hear.

"I want to thank each and every one of you for donating your time today. And to my regular guys, Harry, Hannah, Jessie, you were extraordinary. We saved lives today, dozens of them. Thanks to you, seventeen dogs, one goat, eight rabbits, and thirteen cats found new homes. Not to mention all the kittens back at the shelter. We accomplished something in one day that would normally take an entire year."

Hannah felt her eyes starting to tear up at the thought. They *had* accomplished something great and she was an integral part of it. She had never felt prouder at her achievement.

"So, the tally," Cory said, pausing for dramatic effect. "We raised thirty-one thousand, two hundred, and thirteen dollars. We're staying open for at least another year."

Everyone in the park let out a cheer, hugging whoever was around, and jumping with joy. The shelter was saved. And who knows? Maybe the battle of the bands and dog fashion parade could be a regular event? They could stay open forever, making sure animals always had a safe refuge where they could be cared for and fed without fail. Hannah hoped so, with all her heart, she hoped so.

The celebrations died down as everyone got back to work. They needed their council bond back for the use of the park or their tally would jump down. To do that, they needed to make it pristine.

Yet as they worked now, it was with happy hearts. Somehow the work didn't seem so bad now, even if it was picking up garbage.

Hannah stopped as she saw feet standing on the ground next to her. Her eyes travelled up until they reached Harry's face. "Hey, Harry."

"Hey, can you believe we actually pulled it off? The shelter is going to stay open."

"I know, right? It's fantastic."

Harry paused, looking at her intently. "Jessie told me you organized everything. Why didn't you tell me? I would have helped."

Now it was Hannah's turn to be unable to say what was really on her mind. She had been thinking about it for days, trying to put her finger on why she was feeling so odd. It had come to her during the concert and now the more she thought about it, the more she knew what she had to do.

"Because you *wouldn't* have helped," she started. "You always believed everything Jessie said. You would have been too busy defending her instead of accepting that she got it wrong."

Harry was taken aback, his brows crinkled in confusion. "No, I wouldn't."

"Yes, you would. You've got a blind spot for her, which means you've got a kind heart, but I don't need that right now."

"What are you saying?"

Hannah didn't know if she was brave enough to say the words but it was now or never. "I'm saying I think we should take a break."

She waited in the silence, holding her breath. She didn't know whether she was doing the right thing, she just knew that Harry didn't have her back over the past few weeks and that wasn't okay with her. Hannah knew she would have done anything for him, but it was no good if the respect wasn't mutual.

"Hannah, I don't understand," Harry stuttered out. "What's going on? I thought we were good."

"So did I," Hannah mumbled before leaving. She had to walk away or she knew she would take back the words. She needed some time away from it all, some time to think. Her heart was young and fragile, she couldn't take the knocks to it yet.

❧ The End ❦

A Hairy Tail 4

Dedication

For All Creatures Great and Small.

Chapter 1

Hannah plastered a smile on her face, hoping it didn't look as fake as it felt. She laughed, hoping to convince Veronica and Lucas that she was enjoying herself.

"And the look on the girl's face? It was hilarious," Lucas laughed, recanting the highlights from the movie they had just seen.

"I know, right?" Veronica snorted back, trying to catch her breath.

Hannah subtly checked her watch, seeing if she had stayed long enough to be polite. It wasn't so much that she disliked hanging out with Veronica and Lucas, but normally Harry would be there with them. With the four of them, she had never been the third wheel. Now, she was definitely well ensconced in third wheel territory.

It had been almost an hour since the movie, if she left now, that wouldn't be rude, right? Hannah thought that was a sufficient amount of time. "I have to go, guys," she said as she stood. "I've got a shift at the shelter."

Veronica tore her eyes away from Lucas. "Do they need you anymore? All the animals have been adopted."

"New animals keep coming in, I have to go."

"Okay, have fun." They waved her away and she hurried through the bodies in the mall. It seemed like the entire town was there.

Hannah found her bicycle and unlocked the chain. Jumping on, she headed for home. She didn't have a shift at the shelter, she had barely been there at all in the last week. There was a certain someone she was avoiding and she hadn't seen him since they broke up.

It wasn't like she had abandoned her duties altogether though. After the fundraising concert a week ago, all the animals had been adopted out. The only creatures they now had to look after were any new ones that came in. Hannah had checked in with the manager, Cory, several times to make sure she wasn't needed.

Breaking up with Harry had been the hardest thing Hannah had ever had to do. She didn't want to hurt him, but she didn't like the way she couldn't rely on him to have her back either. Everything she had learned about relationships said that couples were supposed to be a united front, not two separate units.

As a result of the breakup, Hannah had been at a loss with what to do with the rest of the summer. Her mother, Coco, didn't let her mope around the house so that only left hanging out with Veronica. Unfortunately, she was still stuck to Lucas like a rash. At least *her* summer romance was still simmering away.

A text message sounded in Hannah's pocket. She pulled her bicycle over to a stop to check her phone. The message was from Cory, asking her to drop by the shelter.

With a groan, Hannah texted back that she was on her way. At least she wasn't lying to Veronica now. With great trepidation, she cycled toward the shelter. She just prayed Harry and Jessie weren't on the roster to work today.

She didn't get her wish. Two other bikes were chained to the front gate when she arrived. She added her bicycle to the stack and went inside.

The Mapleton Animal Shelter was much quieter than it usually was. Instead of the constant yapping of dogs and meowing of cats, the only noises filling the air were decidedly human.

Hannah went directly to Cory's office. "You asked to see me?"

"Oh, you made it, that was quick," Cory said happily. "I wanted to check in with you and make sure you're okay. You haven't been around much lately. We're starting to get busy again so I need to know if you're still going to be volunteering here."

"I'm fine. I'm definitely still volunteering. I love the animals here."

"Good." Like she always did, Cory avoided getting involved in her volunteer's teenage problems and changed the subject. "Would you have some time now to help us out?"

"Of course." If she was being completely honest, Hannah would have to admit she was about to die of boredom if she had to go home. Doing some manual labor at the shelter was welcome, even if all the cute little kittens had been adopted.

She left Cory and ventured into the animals' room. Most of the cages were completely empty, it made a nice change from the crowded conditions they normally had there.

Seeing Harry half-in a cage made Hannah stop in her tracks. What was she supposed to say to him? How was she supposed to act? She had never had an ex-boyfriend before. It was impossible to know what she should do in the situation.

He pulled himself out too quickly, seeing her standing there frozen before she could move. "Oh, hey Hannah. You back?"

"Yeah, the animals are returning," she said awkwardly. Harry looked just as cute as he always did, it was difficult not racing over to him for a hug. "Cory said she needs another set of hands. That's why I wasn't here last week, she didn't need me."

"I thought it might be because of something else."

The break up sat in the middle of the room like a white elephant. Hannah wondered how long they would have to dance around it before it was directly mentioned. She certainly wasn't going to be the first one to do it anyway. "No, just wasn't needed."

Jessie appeared at the doorway. One look at Hannah and she retreated back outside again, not wanting to interrupt. She went completely unnoticed by the pair.

Hannah's eyes searched around the room, trying to focus anywhere except on Harry. He just stared at her expectantly, like she was supposed to say something. Her eyes fell on a cage unlike any of the others. She had never even seen it before.

"What's in that cage?" She asked, pointing. A whole new sense of dread filled her.

Chapter 2

"An iguana," Harry replied casually, like it wasn't weird to have an exotic lizard in the shelter.

"What's it doing here?"

"Someone found it on the road with an injured foot. They dropped it off here and the vet tended to it."

Hannah slowly approached the cage like the lizard might jump out and attack her at any moment. She expected it to, with its beady eyes and flickering tongue.

She made it to the cage, a piece of plastic lining the wire mesh. So far, it hadn't eaten her. So far, so good. She got a little closer. Close enough to touch it if she wanted to. And Hannah really didn't want to.

"Do you think he's someone's pet or did he come from the wild?" She asked, happy to have something else to focus on.

"Cory thinks he's tame so she suspects he's a pet,"

Harry explained, joining her at the cage. He was standing so close she could feel his breath on her shoulder. She moved a step away.

"How do you lose a pet iguana?"

"I guess he just walks out the door."

Somehow, Hannah thought there would be more to it. It took a special kind of person to have a pet iguana and she figured they wouldn't let it go so easily. "Aren't these things expensive?"

"They can be." Harry wrinkled his brow as he stared at the creature. For the lizard's part, he just stared into space and slid his tongue in and out. "Do you want to touch it?"

"I really don't."

"He's not slimy or anything."

"I'm good," Hannah said, taking another step back to reinforce her words. Touching a lizard was definitely not in her job description – if one existed anyway. "I think I'll go say hi to the dogs or something."

Before she could leave, Harry gently touched her on the arm. "Can we talk... privately, somewhere? Maybe after my shift?"

"I don't think there's any point in that," Hannah said, needing to use all her resolve. "I think we should just both move on."

Disappointment crossed Harry's face. It saddened her like nothing else. Over the summer she had grown used to seeing all the sad looks on the lost animals. Seeing it on the boy she still cared for was most difficult of them all.

He turned his eyes up to meet hers, staring with intensity. "That's fine. But I'm going to win you back,

Hannah. I still have two weeks left of summer and I am going to use every one of those days to make you mine again."

With his words lingering in the air, Harry left in the opposite direction and closed the door behind him. Hannah was left alone, her mouth hanging open in surprise.

As she processed what he said, her lips curled into a smile. Perhaps everything wasn't lost after all. She doubted Harry would be able to do anything to convince her to take him back. That door was closed. Yet it didn't mean he couldn't have some fun trying.

Just as she was about to leave, the door opened again. Harry poked his head back in. "And the iguana needs feeding. It's your turn." The door closed just as abruptly.

Hannah stared at the lizard, her smile now gone. What was she going to do with the thing? She was going to need to do some serious research.

The office was a good distance away from the googly-eyed creature. She fired up the computer and did a web search on 'iguanas'. If she was going to be a veterinarian one day, she was going to have to get used to dealing with more exotic animals.

According to *Love of Lizards*, the online superstore of everything lizard related, Iguanas ate crickets. Hannah imagined feeding him those jumpy little things and almost gagged right then and there.

Surely Cory would have been feeding him something else? Hannah went on a mission in the animal room, searching through all the cupboards to find the iguana's food. It would have been easier to ask Harry, but that was going to be the very last resort. It was also exactly what he expected her to do. She wouldn't make it so easy for him.

The cupboards had lots of supplies, thanks to the fundraising concert. However it didn't appear to have anything for a hungry iguana. At least, nothing was labeled *iguana food*, anyway.

As she was still searching, the door swung open and both Cory and Harry hurried in. She stood up, wondering what all the fuss was about.

Then she saw it. The most horrible, slimy thing that was a hundred times worse than the lizard. Hanging between their arms was a giant green snake.

"Oh my God," Jessie screamed, standing at the back door. "What's that doing here?" If Hannah wasn't frozen in fear, she would probably have screeched the same thing.

"It's just a snake," Harry said calmly. "Someone found it on the road, it's been attacked by something."

Hannah saw the gash on its tail, red and angry. Which probably meant the snake was also angry. As they came further into the room, Hannah retreated backwards until her back was firmly against the wall.

Jessie wasn't sticking around to learn more. All of a sudden she ran across the room, squealing as she hurried toward the office. Hannah couldn't take it any longer, she followed, running as fast as her legs could take her.

"It's just a snake, it's not going to hurt you," Harry called out after them. They were too hysterical to reply. The girls barricaded themselves in the office, locking the door behind them.

"Since when do snakes come in here?" Jessie asked, still shaking with fear.

"That's the first I've seen," Hannah replied. She was trying to calm down, make her heart stop racing in her chest. "First a lizard and now a snake? It's like a madhouse in here. Give me a hundred kittens any day."

"Those things would eat a kitten."

Hannah wasn't going to argue. She had heard stories of giant snakes being able to unlock their jaws and swallow whole animals with one bite. Just the thought of it made her shudder and her skin crawl. The pets she liked were definitely of the hairy variety.

Jessie pulled her cell phone from her pocket. "I'm going to call my mom, I think we're having a family emergency so I can go home early."

While Hannah didn't exactly agree with lying, she wanted to get out of there just as much. "Make sure your mom needs me too."

Chapter 3

Veronica could talk like no-one else Hannah knew. Once she found a topic she liked, her lips moved incessantly until it was out of her system. But that was half her charm. They lazed around her bedroom, enjoying the sun as it streamed in through the windows.

"So Lucas is already talking about going back to school?" Hannah asked. She had just been subjected to almost an hour of Lucas news. Apparently their relationship had only grown stronger over the summer.

Veronica nodded her head eagerly. "We're going to be the hottest new couple in the grade. We can share lunches in the cafeteria, act impossibly cute in front of other couples that aren't as cool, and hold hands between classes."

Hannah resisted the urge to roll her eyes. She disliked couples like that, especially when it wasn't her and Harry. "That's great. I guess the semester will start before we know it."

Sensing a touch of sadness in her best friend, Veronica grew serious. "I'm sorry, I shouldn't be flaunting my wonderful relationship in front of you."

"It's okay, really. It's nice that you've found someone. I like Lucas, he's nice."

"How was seeing Harry the hottie again after you, you know, broke up?"

Hannah could still feel the knot in her stomach that she got every time she thought of him. "Terrible. I didn't know what to say to him."

"Awkward with a capital A?"

She nodded. "But then he went and made it even worse."

Sensing a piece of juicy scandal, Veronica replied eagerly. "What did he do? Tell me he didn't hook up with Jessie the boyfriend stealer."

That *would* have been more awkward, Hannah considered. Thankfully that didn't happen, otherwise she would be out for blood. "No, nothing like that. He said he was going to win me back."

Veronica cocked her head to the side, looking very much like a poodle. "Win you back? Do you even want him back?" She hesitated, just enough to answer her friend's question. "Oh my gosh, you want him back!"

"No, I don't," Hannah insisted. "He upset me and I don't want to give him another chance to do it again. I don't think he even knows what he did wrong."

"He sided with Jessie, I thought that was clear."

"He's a boy, he's not as observant as us."

"I wonder what he's going to do to win you back,"

Veronica mused. "It could be just like the movies. If he stands outside your house with a boom box, please call me so I can come over and watch. I'll record it and put it on YouTube. People eat that kind of stuff up."

"It's not the eighty's," Hannah giggled. "He's not going to even know what a boom box is."

"Fine then, iPod, whatever." She rolled her eyes, unable to remove the cheeky grin from her face before changing the subject. "The bonfire party is coming up next week. I told Lucas you're coming, don't make me a liar."

"I don't want to go by myself."

"You won't be by yourself, you'll have me."

Somehow, that didn't seem as much fun as it would have been to go with Harry. "I'll think about it."

Veronica threw a cushion at her, catching her on the shoulder. "You've been thinking about it for two weeks already. You need to think less and do more."

Hannah threw the cushion back, Veronica caught it. "My shift is going to start soon, I have to go." She got up to leave.

"That's convenient," Veronica called after her.

Hannah was on her bike and peddling to the shelter in no time. The peace of cycling through the streets was welcome after the talk fest.

By the time she walked into the shelter, she was prepared for whatever the animals had in store for her. Well, almost. She had no idea that the place would be overrun with creatures she had never seen before.

"What's going on?" Hannah asked as she walked through the back room. Harry and Cory were working hard trying to fix cages and glass tanks. It was like an exotic pet store had exploded in the room.

"We keep getting more animals dropped off," Cory replied, a green lizard the size of a small cat in her arms. "It's plague proportion now."

Hannah tried to avoid getting too close to any of the cages. She was still worried about where they had put the giant snake from the other day. "Where are they all coming from? Ugh, what is that?"

Harry held up a reptile that looked like a cross between an angry dragon and a baby crocodile. "This is Gus, he's our newest guest here."

"Give me a hand, Hannah," Cory urged. She nodded towards a cage door that needed opening. Trying desperately to stay out of reach, she extended her arm as far as it would go to open the door. She jumped back as Cory pushed the lizard inside. When the door was closed, she was slightly relieved.

"Can I come out now?" Jessie's muffled voice asked from somewhere.

"Yeah, it's in a cage," Cory called back. The door to her office opened and a freaked out looking Jessie joined Hannah by the wall.

"You're such girls," Harry teased as he stroked Gus like he was a dog. There was nothing cute and furry about the creature.

"Where did they all come from?" Hannah asked again, now she was slightly more composed. Her nerves were still on edge, expecting something to jump out at her at any moment.

"People keep bringing them in," Cory explained as she poured what appeared to be worms into a bowl. "Some are injured, others are just weird."

"Is this normal?" Jessie shrieked from her side, her voice way higher than it usually was. Soon, only the dogs would be able to hear her.

Cory laughed. "No, it's not normal. It's anything but. Something weird is going on in Mapleton. I've never seen this many reptiles in one place before."

"You want a pat?" Harry asked, teasing the girls with Gus. They screamed in response, his desired reaction. He laughed away to himself.

Chapter 4

Harry, Hannah, and Jessie sat around the back of the shelter, eating lunch away from the chaos of the animals inside.

"You know," Hannah started. "There could be something big going on with all these weird creatures."

"They're not creatures, they're just animals," Harry corrected her. He earned a grimace for his troubles. "Some people prefer to keep lizards and snakes over cats and dogs."

"Kooks," Jessie snorted. For once, Hannah agreed with the girl. She definitely didn't agree with Harry.

"Fine, there could be something big going on with all these wonderfully cute alternative pets," Hannah continued, adding some sarcasm to the mix.

"Like what?" Harry asked, taking a bite out of his sandwich.

"What about if someone is illegally importing them? They could have gotten loose and they can't report it to the police because it's illegal."

The others shrugged, perhaps. "Why would anyone want to import lizards?" Jessie's face twisted with disgust every time she mentioned them.

"For pets," Harry replied, his frustration growing. Hannah figured it must be a guy thing, surely no girl would be insane enough to like the scaly creatures. "I think your theory might be worth following up. We could also try asking pet stores if they know people trying to sell the animals."

Hannah felt a plan starting to form in her mind. The sooner she worked out what was happening, the sooner they could get the shelter back to normal. And the sooner she could stop jumping at every sound inside.

"We can go after our shift," Harry offered.

Hannah shook her head. "I think this is a job for Jessie and I. What do you think?" She turned her attention to the girl, looking a little surprised at the mention of her name.

Her face lit up. "Sure, I'd love to. Beats sitting around here, waiting to be bitten. Do we keep anti-venom in the first aid kit?"

"They're not venomous," Harry added, suddenly not in such a good mood anymore. He stood to go back inside, his lunch finished. He left the girls to it, seeking solace with the snakes.

Two hours later, Jessie and Hannah were more than relieved to be leaving the shelter. They cleared their investigation with Cory and left on a mission. They needed to get their shelter back.

The first stop was the police station. Cory arranged for them to speak with Officer Edwards. He already knew Hannah from her time in helping them solve a dognapping ring. He would at least take them seriously.

"So, what's up?" Officer Edwards said as he invited them to sit at his desk. They were surrounded by rows of cubicles, each one cluttered with paperwork. The police station was obviously a busy one – and filled with messy people.

"We keep getting lizards and snakes in the shelter," Hannah started. "We wondered if they might be being imported by someone who shouldn't be doing it. Have you heard of anything like that?"

Officer Edwards leant back in his seat, rubbing his chin as he thought it through. Finally, he replied. "We haven't had any reports of missing or stolen reptiles."

Jessie replied eagerly. "We thought they wouldn't report it if they were stolen or illegally imported."

"You're right," the policeman nodded. "But sometimes we hear whispers of things going on. We have informants all over town that keep us in the loop of anything that might be going on."

"Any whispers about animals?" Hannah asked hopefully.

"Afraid not, Miss Wilson. Cory would have been the first person I would have called if we heard something like that."

"Do you get many people importing things illegally here in Mapleton?"

"Sometimes, we do. But they mainly go to Shroveport where there are bigger docks. It's only smaller type vessels that sail into our harbor. A few fish over the allowed limit is the extent of our smuggling operations."

Her shoulders slumped as she tried to think of what else could be causing all the reptiles to end up at the shelter. If they weren't missing or stolen, then how did they all end up out in the open and exposed to injury?

"Have you seen anything like this before?" She finally asked.

Officer Edwards shook his head slowly. "Sorry, it seems a bit of a strange one. Have you checked with the local pet stores?"

"That's next on our list."

"They might have their ear to the ground when it comes to the animal world in Mapleton. With any luck, they'll know of someone missing their private collection of reptiles." He smiled encouragingly.

After making him promise to call Cory if he found anything interesting in his travels, Hannah and Jessie left the policeman alone. Their trip wasn't wasted altogether, at least they had another set of eyes trying to solve the mystery.

As they picked up their bicycles, Jessie looked at her watch. "The pet stores will be closed by the time we get there. Do you want to grab a cold drink on the way back to the shelter?"

Hannah hadn't realized how long they had been waiting to see Officer Edwards. Racing back to the shelter didn't seem that appealing. "Sure, why not? Harry loves all the snakes, it won't hurt him to be alone with them for a while longer."

They rode to the nearest corner store and purchased an ice cold soda each. Sitting on the seat outside, Hannah realized she had never truly been alone with Jessie before. She didn't know what to say to the girl.

Thankfully, Jessie didn't have a problem talking. "It sucks that summer is almost over. It's going to be weird going back to school."

Hannah didn't mind school, she relished the learning part. However, the socializing, the events, the bullies, she could do without. "I guess summer can't last forever."

"Nothing really lasts forever."

Something in her wistful tone made Hannah instantly think about Jessie's parent's divorce. She would have assumed the girl would be happy to get back to a routine so she didn't have to think about it all the time. "How are your parents going?"

A sadness flooded Jessie's face. "My dad moved out last week. It's just me and my mom now."

"Sorry."

"Harry said your parents are divorced too?"

Hannah nodded, remembering the day her father had moved out. She stayed in her room all day, refusing to believe it was happening. With his last box loaded into the car, she had watched him drive away from her window. "For almost three years now."

"Does it get easier?" Jessie asked hopefully.

"I guess it depends on your parents. I don't see my dad very much but my mom is great to me. She can be really annoying, but she's my dad too, in a way."

"My dad used to call me his princess." She stared into the street, trying to blink back the tears. "He promised to stay in touch and that we'd see each other all the time."

Hannah remembered her father saying the same thing. Then he moved to a big town two hour's drive away. The occasional phone call on her birthday or at

Christmas was all she got now. Still, she didn't want to make Jessie any more upset than she already was. Divorce was hard, she wasn't going to make it any harder.

"I'm sure your dad will do as he says," Hannah said, even though she didn't believe it. "You'll probably see more of him now because he'll feel guilty for not living with you and seeing you every day at breakfast."

The edge of Jessie's mouth twisted into a smile. "I hope so. My mom kind of gets involved in her own stuff. She forgets I'm there sometimes. Did your dad remarry? Do you have brothers and sisters?"

"He lives with a woman who has two kids – a boy and a girl. They don't have any children together."

"Do you like them? Or is she really mean to you?"

Hannah hadn't spent enough time with them to actually form an opinion. Her father liked to keep his new life very separate. "I guess they're okay."

A momentary silence settled over them, both girls thinking about the divorce and how their lives could have been different if things didn't end badly between their parents.

"We should get back," Hannah finally sighed. "But if you ever want to talk about anything, just let me know."

Jessie couldn't resist giving her a hug. "Thank you." They got back on their bikes and headed to the shelter.

Chapter 5

"Come on, little ones, we've got to get back," Hannah called out to the half dozen dogs she had running around her feet.

A fluffy black poodle cross jumped up, leaning on her knee and staring into her eyes. Hannah thought for sure that if he could talk, he would be asking for some more time to play.

"Oh, go on then, another few minutes," she replied to his silent question.

Hannah didn't have the heart to corral them in just yet. She was a sucker for the animals and they knew it. But it wasn't much letting them expend all their energy before having to go back to their cages. She let them enjoy their freedom.

Glancing through the window of the shelter, she could see Harry cleaning out the cage of the iguana. The lizard remained completely still while he did it, as if pretending he would be invisible if he just didn't move. Hannah figured that was kind of cute. Perhaps the creatures weren't as bad as she had thought. As for Harry, she still wasn't so sure.

After another half hour, she finally got the dogs back into the cages. Her shift had ended an hour ago but that didn't matter. She said goodbye to everyone and rode home.

The weather was still perfect for the summertime, hot days and balmy nights. Hannah tried to enjoy it as much as she could. That probably included going to the bonfire party, but she wasn't so sure of that either. She would have to delay Veronica for a little while yet.

Arriving home, Hannah rifled through her handbag for some lip gloss, her pout chapped from the sun. As her hand clasped around the tube, there was something else in her bag.

She pulled out a folded piece of paper, unable to recall putting it in there. She often wrote notes to herself to remind her about things, but she couldn't remember doing that recently.

The note wasn't in her handwriting but she did recognize the scrawl. Harry had been the one to put pen to paper. She read through:

You looked beautiful today, you took my breath away.

No matter how many times she read it, the words didn't change. Nor did it change the way it made her heart beat just a little bit faster.

It was sweet, but just a note. She couldn't fall in love with Harry all over again because of a note. It wasn't going to happen, no way. She replaced it in her handbag and tried to forget about it.

Coco was outside with Billy, throwing him the ball and then having to retrieve it herself. Billy never liked giving up the ball when he had chased after it. There was something about the game of fetch he just didn't get.

"Hey, honey, how was your day?" Coco asked, sitting on the decking for a break.

"Pretty good."

"Still lots of slithery thing?"

Hannah nodded and sat beside her. She was all too aware that it was the same place her and Harry had sat together only a few weeks earlier. "Lots. They freak me out."

"I tend to find the things that freak me out are the things I don't fully understand."

She let the words sink in, they actually sounded pretty logical. "So you think I should get to know the animals?"

"It couldn't hurt. Face your fears," Coco said resolutely. "Is anything else bothering you?"

The note instantly flashed into Hannah's mind. She didn't know if her mother would make a big deal out of it if she brought it up. She played it safe instead, perhaps Veronica would be better for love advice. "What was your first love like?"

Coco's eyes glazed over as she delved into the past. "His name was Drew Schenty and I thought he was the grooviest dude on the planet."

"Did you date him?"

"Of course I did, I was quite groovy myself back then. We would hang out at the beach or at the drive-in cinema. We would share milkshakes and laugh at nothing."

Despite the generation gap, Hannah could imagine her mother as a teenager. She was probably more like Veronica than herself, but the image made her smile anyway. "Were you together long?"

"About a month."

"Only a month?" She had made it sound like it was an eternity, two connected souls forever entwined. "What happened?"

"I found somebody else I liked better," Coco laughed. "Young love is fleeting."

"But you said you loved him."

She nodded her head happily. "And I did. I loved him until I found someone else to love. The point is, Hannah, you're so young you are going to fall in love with a lot of boys before you find the one you know is really the one for you. Harry is your Drew. You'll always remember the way he made you feel and you'll always smile about it. But you won't miss him forever."

Her words were starting to sink in. "So you think I should get over Harry?"

Coco rubbed her back in comfort, just like she had done since Hannah was a baby. "I think you're old enough to make your own decisions. If you feel like your time with Harry isn't over, then you owe it to both of you to address it. If you think it is over, then be kind and move on. Boy's hearts are fragile too."

"Harry wants to get back together," she blurted out, not entirely meaning to.

"How does that make you feel?"

"Scared. But a part of me is excited about it too. It's like nauseous butterflies, they're not all good." Billy stood in front of her, nuzzling her hands for a pat. She absentmindedly pet him. "What do you think I should do?"

"Hannah, I'm not going to tell you what to do. Just do what you think is right. You'll work it out," Coco answered as she stood. "I'm going to put something on for dinner. Make sure Billy has used up all his energy before coming inside."

Once alone, Hannah pulled Billy onto her lap, giving him a hug. "Why can't boys be more like you? Huh, boy?"

He gave her an all-knowing look before settling in for the cuddle.

Chapter 6

"This is getting ridiculous," Jessie moaned as they left another pet store. "I didn't know Mapleton had so many places to buy animals."

Hannah was growing tired of their endless search too but wasn't going to complain about it. She didn't want to sound like Jessie. They had already been to a dozen pet stores and nobody knew of any reptiles that had gone missing or been sold illegally. It was turning into a wild goose chase.

"There's only a few more to go," Hannah pointed out. "If it means getting rid of all the snakes and lizards at the shelter, I'll go to a hundred stores."

Jessie shrugged, agreeing. "Why couldn't we be overrun with bunnies or something? Why slithery things?"

"We're just lucky, I guess."

They entered the next store on their list, printed first thing that morning by Cory. The girls were not much use to her at the shelter, part of the task was to keep them busy and out of her hair. If something came from it, then it was a bonus.

The man behind the counter seemed friendly enough, greeting them as the buzzer on the door sounded. "Hey, girls. What can I do for you?"

Hannah took the lead. "We work at the Mapleton Animal Shelter. We have had a bunch of snakes and lizards come in that people have found. We're asking all the pet stores if they know of anyone missing some reptiles?"

He rubbed his chin as he thought about it. "No-one's come looking, no. But I have had to order in some special snake food for a customer."

"Someone asked for it especially?"

He nodded, he kind of looked like an old Zac Efron. "I don't normally have snake food, there isn't a real demand for it in Mapleton. But this guy came in and said he had run out and really needed it fast."

Jessie and Hannah exchanged a glance. At least it was something, more than they had received from any of the other pet stores. "I don't suppose you could tell us his address so we could talk to him?" Hannah asked, not really expecting a good answer.

"I shouldn't."

Jessie stepped a little closer, smiling like an absolutely innocent little girl. "We just want to find the owners of the snakes we have, that's all. Please help us? We promise not to tell them where we got the address."

His eyes flicked between the two girls. Hannah plastered on her best smile, the one that usually got her out of trouble with Coco. It worked about eighty percent of the time.

Finally, he sighed. "I guess I could read it out loud. If you happen to overhear, then I can't do anything about that. Hold on a second."

Hannah made a mental note, you could get what you wanted from the male persuasion if you smiled at them enough. That might come in handy later on.

After typing painfully slow into his computer. The man took a deep breath. "840 Somerton Road, Mapleton," he read off. He pretended to see the girls standing there for the first time. "My, I didn't see you there. I hope you didn't overhear me."

Jessie giggled. "Of course not. Thank you for your help."

"I hope you find the owners," he called after them.

To be thorough, the girls continued on to the remaining pet stores. Partly because they wanted to do a good job, partly because they didn't want to return to the shelter.

None of the other stores had unusual sales of exotic pet food or knew of any missing animals. Or, if they did, they weren't talking to them. Hannah and Jessie left the last store with nothing but sore feet and a quickly fading determination.

"Should we check out this address?" Hannah asked as she held up the small slip of paper.

Jessie shrugged, indifferent. "I guess if it means not having to go back and wrangle with those slimy snakes, then yes I think we should."

They hopped on their bikes and peddled across town. In the heat of the day, it was nice feeling the wind in their hair. If nothing else, at least the cycling was keeping them fit. Wasn't Coco always going on about Hannah needing to get outside more?

The girls pulled up at the address, confused. "Are you sure this is the right place?" Jessie asked, looking around at the empty field.

Hannah checked the address for the ninth time, comparing the handwritten details to the stenciled number on the curb. "This is definitely it. There's nothing here."

"Absolutely nothing."

"Unless grass counts."

"It doesn't," Jessie stated simply. "If there were snakes here, then they've gone now."

"Perhaps they got their address confused?" Hannah suggested, not really believing it herself. Who doesn't know where they live? Even a five year old knows that.

"Or they gave the pet store a bogus address on purpose." Jessie wasn't as optimistic as her friend. "If you were doing something wrong, you'd give the incorrect address so they couldn't trace you."

"Like something illegal."

"If I was going to break the law, I wouldn't do it with snakes and lizards. Uck." She shivered with the thought, her face twisted in disgust. Her look made Hannah start giggling, did she look like that when Harry talked about the lizards? She hoped not, that would be embarrassing.

"Come on, let's get back and tell Cory about our wild goose chase," Hannah said as she jumped back on her bike. Jessie followed, albeit a little more reluctantly.

To slow the pace and delay the inevitable return to the slimy and slithery animals, Jessie started talking. Hannah had no choice except to keep pace with her. "Are you going to the bonfire party on the beach?"

Hannah inwardly moaned, was everyone obsessed with the party of the summer? "I don't know. I was going to go with Harry and I don't want to go alone now, so I guess not."

"I was sorry to hear you guys broke up," Jessie replied, an honesty ringing in her voice. "I hope it wasn't because of me. I know I was kind of a cow when I first started at the shelter."

"It wasn't because of you, we just weren't what I was hoping for."

"Harry's a really nice guy. I know he's upset about what happened. Even though I don't know what went on, I think you should give him another shot."

Hannah wanted to pedal faster to avoid the conversation but she didn't want to be so obvious. "It was just a summer romance, I'm sure he'll get over it once school starts again."

"He said he'd never felt so much for someone before you," Jessie continued. "If someone said that about me, I would die."

"Did he put you up to this?" Hannah asked, suddenly suspicious. One minute Harry says he's going to try to win her back and then Jessie the boyfriend stealer lays on the guilt trip? Surely it couldn't be a coincidence.

Jessie's mouth dropped open in shock. "No, of course not. I don't talk to him about you, I just listen. We're not all that close."

"You spend a lot of time together for not being *that* close."

"We're neighbors. And home alone a lot. It's a convenience thing."

Hannah didn't know how much of that to believe.

She let the topic drop, she didn't have any desire to be Jessie's best friend and share her deepest thoughts with her. They were colleagues, that was all.

In the silence, however, Jessie wasn't going to give up. "You know, I don't have anyone to go to the bonfire party with either. Maybe we could go together?"

Why was it so important for her to go to the bonfire party? Hannah wondered what kind of a conspiracy there was against her. She gave Jessie the same answer she had given Veronica: "I'll think about it."

Chapter 7

Hannah had been trying to ignore Harry for a good ten minutes and it wasn't working. She knew she had to say something to him, she had to bring up the note he left in her handbag but didn't know what to say. How did you start a conversation like that?

Her eyes had been flicking between Harry and Lulu the dog since she got back to the shelter. With only two hours left of her shift, she didn't have much time left to confront him. And if there was something Hannah disliked, it was confrontation.

She returned Lulu to her cage. It was now or never. "I got your note yesterday."

Harry didn't look at her, his eyes remained fixated on the snake cage he was cleaning. "What note?" He asked casually.

"You know the one." She wasn't buying it, she knew him too well.

He finally stopped his intense scrubbing and turned

to her. "Oh, *that* note. I meant every word of it."

"Maybe you should see a doctor if your breath was taken away. Perhaps your asthma is playing up again."

Harry grinned. "I don't think it was the asthma." He pulled an inhaler out of his pocket and waved it around. "I've got that covered. It was definitely you that took my breath away."

She had to fight every urge to just forgive him already and wrap herself in his arms. She knew she couldn't let him know that. "I think you'll have to try harder next time. A note isn't going to cut it."

He laughed. "The note was stage one. You better prepare yourself for some awesomeness headed your way. It's going to be epic."

Hannah rolled her eyes, playfully teasing him. "Sure, whatever."

They stared at each other for a few electricity charged moments. Hannah could feel her heart pounding in her chest, the way only Harry could make it act.

Finally, Harry broke the silence. "Do you want to help with Monty? I could use another set of hands to move him."

Her eyes flicked between the boy and the snake. Knowing it had a cute name like Monty didn't make it any easier. Yet she remembered how much she wanted to be a vet and that would probably involve a snake at some stage in her career. She had to do it, she found herself nodding.

"Great, come here," Harry replied happily. He held the back part of the snake out of the glass cage. "Slide your hands under here, right where my hands are."

Every instinct in Hannah's body told her to run.

34

She ignored the screaming in her head and did as she was told. The snake wasn't slimy like she thought it would be. Instead, it was smooth and warmer than she expected. If she forgot it was a snake, it wasn't so bad at all.

"I'm going to get the head and then we'll lift him up and out. He has to go into that cage over there. Got it?" Harry pointed towards the glass enclosure across the room. It looked a lot further away than it really was. "We can't drop him. You can do this, Han, I know you can."

"Let's just get it over and done with."

"Okay," he grinned. "One, two, three." On the third count they heaved the heavy snake out of the cage and started to shuffle across the room.

Harry held the snake's head in front of him so Hannah couldn't see it. Even though she could feel the snake contract in her hands, she could pretend it was just a rope or something. Still, the sooner she was finished, the better.

He gently lowered the creature into the large tank and continued to hold its head until Hannah had released the back half and stepped away. Only then did he release it and secure the lid.

"Well done," he congratulated her.

"I touched a snake. I moved a snake." She stared at her hands, wanting to wash them. "I did it. I did it!" Without thinking, she wrapped her arms around Harry's neck and gave him a squeeze.

He hugged her back, deciding not to care that it was only a spur of the moment thing and it didn't mean anything.

The moment Hannah realized what she had done,

she let him go. "Sorry."

"Don't be," he laughed. "You're going to make a great vet one day."

As his words lingered in the air, Harry headed towards the storage room for his next errand. Hannah was left alone, with at least a dozen reptiles for company. She was planted on the spot, not knowing what had just happened.

Hugging Harry didn't mean she still had feelings for him, right? It just meant she was happy at her accomplishment and that's all there was to it. She desperately tried to believe her own lies.

The iguana in the tank next to the snake blinked at her with those beady eyes she used to find so repugnant. "Don't look at me like that," she warned him. The way he stared was disconcerting. She thought for sure she knew what he was thinking. "Stop judging me. I can't let him back in. He hurt me. I can't do it again."

The iguana blinked again, turning his head elsewhere as something more interesting caught his attention. Hannah shook her head and headed towards the sink to rid herself of snake germs.

Chapter 8

"It's summer," Veronica pointed out bluntly, and a little sarcastically. "We are obligated to go to the beach at least once while on summer vacation. It's a law or something."

Hannah wasn't so sure. She didn't feel comfortable in her swimsuit, even if it was a one piece that covered everything it had to. Looking around at all the perfect bodies with not one wobbly bit in sight, she didn't think she would be able to take off her light cotton wrap.

Veronica obviously didn't feel the same way as she peeled off her dress and showed the tiniest bikini Hannah had ever seen.

"You're wearing less than underwear," she said in a panic. She had to fight the urge to cover her with a towel before anyone saw.

Veronica just shrugged. "I guess it depends what kind of underwear you wear. It's not smaller than mine." She looked Hannah up and down pointedly. "Probably smaller than yours."

"Smaller than half of mine," Hannah giggled, she would have liked even a tiny fraction of her friend's confidence. "What are we going to do here?"

Veronica sighed dramatically. "Relax, that's what we're going to do. You and I are going to sit here, enjoy the ocean, the seagulls, the sun, and the boys." She nodded towards a group of boys from school as they kicked a ball around – shirtless.

Hannah tried to relax. She leant back and stretched her legs, feeling the warm sand run through her toes. As she looked out at the sea, all she could think of was the last time she had been there. It was with Harry when they were on their first date. They had been completely saturated by that ocean water and then giggled uncontrollably about it. The thought still made her smile.

No matter how much she tried not to think of him, he always found a way to worm inside her head again. She knew it wasn't his fault, but she blamed him anyway. If he hadn't told her he wanted her back, she would have been able to move on. At least, that was her theory anyway.

"Earth to Hannah, come in, hello," Veronica's voice forced her way into her daydream. Hannah shook her head and gave her friend her full attention. "Check out the clown."

"You shouldn't call people clowns, it's not very nice."

"No, seriously, check out the *clown*."

She followed her pointed finger and spotted the man dressed as a clown halfway down the beach. His bright orange hair was twice as wide as his shoulders. Even in the hot sand he was wearing oversized red shoes that were bigger than flippers.

"Clowns are creepy," Hannah said, unable to tear her eyes away from the sight. He was getting closer as he handed flyers out to people.

"I know, right?"

"Whoever came up with them was weird. I wonder how they even thought that a guy dressed like that could entertain people?"

"Freak, right?" Hannah shrugged, agreeing. They continued to watch the clown until he was standing in front of them. Up close, his white face makeup was cracked and dripping in the heat. He looked like a melting wax candle.

"Hey girls," he greeted them, shoving a flyer in each of their hands. "The Big Top Circus is in town, come along and enjoy the spectacular acrobats, animals, and clowns." He squeezed his bulbous red nose which honked before leaving.

Hannah scanned the flyer, having no intention of seeing any more clowns. Even in their own habitat with festive music and acrobats, they wouldn't be any less creepy. Still, she couldn't help feel sorry for the poor guy, he must have been sweltering in that outfit on the hot sand. She carefully folded the flyer and slipped it into her bag.

After another few hours of spending the obligatory time on the sand, Hannah was ready for home. "Want to grab some lunch?"

"I could eat," Veronica nodded. They packed up their things and started the walk into the town centre. It was normally only a short trip, but in the heat of the midday sun, it was taking way too long. Hannah tried to stay off the road, taking shelter in the shade of the trees.

"What are you doing? You're going to get yourself lost," Veronica warned, obviously not feeling the effects of the sun like her friend.

"I need some shade, I'm going to burn."

"A tan never hurt anyone."

"Yeah, actually skin cancer kills thousands of people every day," Hannah shot back. "I think that classifies as hurting people."

"Whatever," she rolled her eyes and subtly moved into the shade with her.

They continued walking along the quiet street, the only cars being the occasional beachgoer either coming or going.

As she walked, Hannah thought she heard footsteps. She couldn't tell where they were coming from exactly, but there was definitely rustling amongst the trees.

All of a sudden, the rustling was punctuated with a high pitched screech, making both the girls jump. "What was that?" Veronica squealed, jumping closer to Hannah.

"I don't know," she replied, stopping to look around. She ignored Veronica's tugging on her arm and headed toward the noise.

They crept along together slowly, all their senses on high alert. Hannah couldn't even imagine what had made the sound but she would put her money on some kind of animal. Hopefully a species that didn't hurt humans.

Something moved amongst the trees, making them

stand as still as a statue. The figure stopped too, just as scared of them. A little brown creature with huge brown eyes stared at them.

"It's a monkey," Hannah said in disbelief.

"What's a monkey doing in Mapleton?" Veronica asked, standing slightly behind her friend for safety. She wasn't the one who loved all creatures great and small.

"I don't know, but he might be hurt." Hannah took a slow and deliberate step forward, making no sudden movement to scare the poor thing.

The huge eyes watched her every move, not letting her get away with anything. She continued on, trying not to startle him. "It's okay, I'm not going to hurt you. Are you hurt? Are you lost?"

The monkey didn't have any answers for her. However, as soon as she got in reaching distance, he took off running in the opposite direction.

Hannah ran after him, there was no way she could leave him in the suburban area by himself. Monkeys didn't just turn up in Mapleton on their own, just like snakes and iguanas didn't.

"What are you doing?" Veronica called out.

"We can't let him go!" Hannah yelled back, trying not to lose sight of the little scamp. She ran through the trees, slowly closing the gap between her and the animal. A few times she made a jump for the monkey but each time he eluded her grasp.

In a desperate hope to escape, the monkey hurried up a tree. It clung to the branches, holding on for dear life. Hannah stood at the bottom, trying to remember the last time she had climbed a tree. She wasn't sure she ever had.

Veronica finally caught up, puffing. "Now what do we do?"

"We get him down, his little hand is injured. Look, it's bleeding." She pointed to the monkey's left front hand. "We have to get it to a vet. It's probably hungry too. Hold my bag, I'm going up."

She shoved her beach gear into Veronica's hands and made sure her sandshoes were secured to her feet before starting the climb. The bark of the tree was loose, the leaves scratchy, and she knew it definitely wasn't designed for people to climb up.

Still, she pushed herself onwards, not looking down. If there was one thing she hated more than climbing the tree, it was falling from the tree. She gripped a little tighter with the thought.

Finally, with no skin left on her knees and hands, she reached the branch she needed. The monkey was trapped, he couldn't go down or up. "Hey there, little guy, I'm going to get you some help. You can trust me."

The big eyes just stared at her, shaking a little with fear. Hannah slowly reached out and grabbed him, cradling the little bundle close to her chest. He didn't struggle much, which only made her certain he was more injured than he appeared to be.

Sitting on the branch, there was one thing Hannah hadn't considered – how to actually get down while holding the monkey.

"Vee, can you please empty my beach bag and throw it up? I'll put him inside," she called down. Veronica did as instructed and dumped the contents of the bag onto the ground. It took a few throws, but Hannah eventually caught it. Careful not to hurt him any more than he already was, she gently placed the monkey into the bag and zipped it shut. It was made of cotton and would allow him to breathe for a while yet.

Hannah secured the bag over her back and climbed down. It was a relief to be back on solid ground again. "We need to get him to the shelter, Cory will call the vet."

Chapter 9

Hannah stood by the stainless steel bench and carefully watched the vet, Brady, as he looked over the monkey. He had already identified it as a Capuchin monkey, definitely not native to the region.

"He appears to be well looked after," Brady commented. "Besides the busted hand, of course. Hold this." He handed Hannah the monkey's arm as he rifled around for some supplies.

"Will his hand heal?" She asked, feeling the warmth of the little creature in her fingers. Now he was sedated, she could get a better look at him. His round little face was neatly clipped, his coat shiny and soft. He looked so cute she had to resist the urge to scoop him up in her arms and cradle him like he was a baby.

Brady found what he was looking for and started to tend to the wound. "It will heal fine and be just like new. He's lucky he didn't get hit by a car or something worse. I wonder where he came from? Hold still, he might move when I start putting the antiseptic on the wound."

Hannah held the hand in the palm of her open one, her other hand stroking his head gently. She wanted to make the animal feel safe and give him comfort. She imagined he must be terrified about being in a strange place with unknown humans.

Brady moved swiftly over the wound, his capable hands applied the cream and then bandaged the monkey's hand without fuss.

"Cory tells me you want to be a vet when you're older," Brady started, making conversation in the otherwise quiet room.

"I really do."

"Well, I've seen what you do here at the shelter, and I can say you're going to make an awesome vet one day. Don't give up on your dream." He smiled kindly and finished up as Hannah beamed back at him.

She watched in awe as he placed the monkey in a cage, waiting for him to wake up. All Hannah could think of was how much she wanted to be like him one day. She imagined herself looking after the animal, healing his pain. She knew she would be able to do it, that she would be that capable one day too. To hear the reassurance from Brady's lips was like a dream.

"Do you really think I'll make a good vet?" She asked again, hoping she didn't imagine it.

"You love animals, that's a good start. But, above all, you're gentle with them. They already trust you, instinctively they know you're not going to hurt them. It all points to a born vet to me." Brady patted her on the shoulder before busying himself with the monkey.

Hannah left him to check in with Cory. She had

been on the phone trying to track down any reports of a missing Capuchin. They all knew there was no chance a well cared for monkey could just be wandering the streets of Mapleton alone.

She waited patiently while Cory finished up her phone call. Only then did she turn to Hannah. "The police haven't heard anything."

"Does that mean it could be illegally owned?" Hannah asked.

Cory shrugged. "Maybe, or it could just be too early for the report to come through. If the little guy only went missing this morning, the owners might still be looking for him. I'll get something online to get the word out."

"Does that mean we can go home now?" Veronica moaned from the chair in the hallway. Hannah was surprised she had waited around for that long.

Hannah glanced at Cory. "Go home, it's not your shift today. We have plenty of volunteers to help out. I promise to call if anything happens with the patient."

Veronica stood, grabbing her hand. "See? The boss says to go, so we better get going."

"Can I come?" They turned around to see Jessie standing in the doorway. She was already taking off her apron. "My shift is over."

Hannah didn't want to be rude, she couldn't very well turn around and say no. Especially when she had an audience. "We're probably just going to hang out at home for the afternoon."

"I don't mind," Jessie said happily.

"Okay, then," Hannah forced a smile as Veronica shot her a look. She would hear all about her terrible decision when they were alone later, no doubt.

The three girls left the shelter and walked to Hannah's house, grabbing an ice cream at the corner shop along the way. By the time they arrived, the afternoon sun was forcing them indoors.

They sat around Hannah's bedroom, sipping on ice tea and watching Billy go crazy with so many people to pet him. He didn't know which lap to curl up in first.

"This dog is crazy," Veronica giggled, trying to stop the pooch's tongue licking her face clean.

"He's crazy cute," Jessie cooed. "Did you get him from the shelter?"

Hannah nodded. "Yeah, Cory gave him to me. He's fit in perfectly here."

"Crazy, just like your mom," Veronica teased. Hannah laughed, she couldn't disagree. They were all a little mad in the Wilson household.

Jessie changed the subject. "Harry was working at the shelter today, he said he was planning something big for you."

Hannah's ears pricked up, desperate to know the details but not wanting *them* to know that. She tried to pretend she didn't care. "Oh, really? It's probably something lame."

"He was pretty excited about it," she shrugged.

Veronica's smile could not be contained. "Harry the hottie has something planned? Oooh, give me all the deets Jess, I need details."

Jessie's eyes came alive, delighted to be able to gossip. "He said Hannah's going to love it because it's perfect for her. I begged him for specifics and he just said that I wouldn't be able to keep the secret. He said no girl can keep a secret for more than ten minutes."

Hannah inwardly laughed, he had said the same

thing to her before too. He was kind of right, maybe not on the ten minute timeframe but definitely the secrets thing. Wouldn't Jessie have spilled everything if she knew more?

Veronica looked scandalized. "Harry the hottie has a secret. We have to find out what he's planning."

"We could follow him," Jessie suggested. "He doesn't have to know we're doing it."

"We could wear disguises," Veronica agreed.

Hannah wasn't going to have a bar of it. "We won't be doing anything. If Harry thinks some gimmick surprise will get me back, then he's mistaken. Can we please change the subject?"

She stared both the girls down, challenging them to say another thing about Harry. Both Jessie and Veronica knew better.

Veronica sighed. "So the bonfire party. Are you in or out, Hannah?"

It wasn't the change of subject Hannah was hoping for. She crossed her arms, thinking. The party was only a few days away, she was hoping time would just run out and she would conveniently forget to attend. That was the plan, but the more she was hassled about it, the less likely that was going to work.

"Come with me," Jessie said in the silence. "We can go together, please? Don't let me go alone like a Nigel no friends."

"Come on Hans, you have to be there," Veronica begged. "You won't even notice you don't have a date."

"I'll be her date."

Hannah finally relented. "Fine. If it means you'll both stop nagging me, then I'll go.

"Yeah!" They exclaimed together, finally winning the battle.

Hannah was already dreading the bonfire party. She wasn't entirely sure why, but she had a bad feeling about it. She wasn't one to trust her gut instinct, she preferred to put her faith in logic and reason. This feeling was entirely a new one.

Chapter 10

Her dress was ironed, her hair neatly pulled back into a ponytail, she even had a brushing of makeup on. All the ingredients were there for Hannah to feel amazing but she couldn't stop worrying.

"Oh my God, this looks awesome," Jessie muttered under her breath. For the bonfire party, she had chosen more sequins than was appropriate for the beach but she didn't seem to care.

She grabbed Hannah's hand and pulled her through the crowd of moving bodies. Teenagers of all ages danced to the thumping music being spun by a DJ set up across from the bonfire. The only lighting came from the fire and a set of torches set up at regular intervals.

Everybody was laughing and talking around them, it seemed the only one not having a good time was Hannah. And that's how she felt too.

"Maybe I should go," she started, yelling to be

heard. "You'll have more fun without me."

"What? I can't hear you?" Jessie tugged her ear to reiterate her point. Except, she *could* hear her, she was just choosing not to listen. The begging to go home had grown old in the car on the way there. Far better she just ignore Hannah.

They spotted Veronica and Lucas dancing on the sand, the lights from the fire dancing over them. Veronica waved over her boyfriend's shoulder when she saw them. The beaming smile on her face betrayed the fun she was having.

"Dance with me," Jessie insisted. She moved Hannah's hands for her, clunking away to the beat. "Try to have some fun, it's not going to hurt. I promise."

Hannah felt herself relax – a little. Jessie's enthusiasm was catching, no matter what she did to resist. She felt guilty for disliking her so much when they had first met only a few weeks ago.

They bopped along to the music, quickly getting overwhelmed with the heat of the fire and the summer night. "Do you want a drink?" Hannah asked. Jessie nodded and she stalked off to the drinks vendor.

The line seemed to take forever but it was worth it for the cold soda. Hannah searched through the crowds to find Jessie talking with Veronica and Lucas. She handed the girl her drink.

"It's great to see you, Han," Lucas greeted her happily. His arm was around Veronica's back, it was nice to see them so happy together. Maybe all summer romances weren't just for the summer, Hannah thought to herself.

"You too, Lucas. Everyone having fun?" She

received three head nods in reply. "Is it always this crowded?"

Veronica looked around. "It seems a bit bigger than last year. I guess more people are hearing about it now."

Hannah took a breath to reply but stopped when someone tapped her on the shoulder. She quickly spun around to see who everyone was looking at behind her.

Harry grinned, his blue eyes drilling into her. "Hey Hannah. You want to dance?"

She did but she didn't too. Dancing with Harry was fun, it had been every time. When she was with him, she didn't feel like the clumsy, self-conscious fool she normally was. Harry turned her from the ugly duckling into the beautiful swan, at least that's the best way she could describe it.

"Go on, Han," Jessie urged, Veronica giving her a subtle push into Harry's arms. He seized the opportunity and pulled her onto the dance floor.

Hannah let her feet and body move but she didn't want to put her heart into it. Harry was too cute, he smelled too good, and he made her feel special when she let her guard down. She couldn't let him back in and give him permission to break her heart again.

"The monkey's doing better," Harry said out of the blue, trying to make it less awkward.

"He's up and about again?"

"Yeah. Cory's having trouble keeping him from being bored. I think she'd like to open the door and let him go free," he joked, his eyes sparkling in the firelight. Hannah desperately tried not to notice.

"Maybe that's how he got into the situation to

begin with," she suggested.

The music stopped and went down to a slower pace, *A Thousand Years* by Christina Perri played. Harry moved closer to wrap his arms around her. She let him, sinking into his chest. If she closed her eyes, it was like they had never broken up in the first place. She could forget about what happened and pretend everything was perfect.

"You look really pretty tonight," Harry whispered against her hair. "I'm glad you came."

She didn't reply, just continued on with the side to side movements that passed as dancing. She felt herself melting into Harry, the way she used to. It felt so good to be in his arms and he was wearing her favorite cologne. The overall effect was making her giddy.

The song finished and changed to *Live While We're Young* by One Direction, breaking the spell. Hannah tore herself away from Harry, shaking her head. "I have to go."

"No, Hannah, stay with me," Harry called out, trying to follow her.

Hannah pushed through the bodies, most of them dancing happily without a care in the world. All the couples looked like they belonged together. She wondered if her and Harry looked the same? She couldn't bear the thought.

The couples only added to Hannah's unease. She shouldn't have come, she was a science nerd, she didn't belong at teenage parties. And she certainly shouldn't have been in Harry's arms when she had vowed to protect her heart. Boys were trouble, they only led to confusion and pain.

She broke away from the crowd, stopping in the shadows of the outskirts of the party. Harry was right behind her, still insisting she stop.

Hannah spun around, the tears stinging her eyes. "I can't do this Harry, I can't be here. This isn't me."

"It's only a party. What's wrong?" His brow was wrinkled with confusion. He still made her heart speed up, which was very much a problem.

"I don't want to be with you. I mean, I do, but I don't. So I have to go." She pulled her cell phone out of her pocket, dialing Coco with shaking hands. She felt for sure she sounded as crazy to other people as she did with her own ears.

Harry waited patiently while she asked Coco to pick her up straight away. He didn't try to stop her, he wouldn't prevent her from doing anything she so obviously wanted. Only when she hung up, did he speak again.

"Hannah, I'm sorry if I upset you," he said gently.

"You didn't, you didn't do anything. It's me, I just can't handle this. It was supposed to be a simple summer and then it got... complicated."

"I'm glad I spent the summer with you. I would rather that than a thousand simple summers."

Hannah bit her bottom lip, trying to stop it quivering. It would be so easy just to throw her arms around his neck and forgive him. She was having trouble even remembering why she was so upset with him in the first place.

Harry took a step closer, making it even easier for her to reach him. Still, she stayed where she was. "Hannah, I'm so sorry. I want you back so much, I love you. I'm so new at this whole boyfriend thing, I didn't mean to make mistakes. I'm still learning."

He moved close enough to rest his forehead against hers. He took her hands in his, holding them tightly so she couldn't get away.

Hannah was acutely aware of how close he was. All she had to do was angle her head slightly and their lips would meet. Just a tiny movement, that's all it would take. She could stop the ache in her heart, she could forget the last few weeks happened. Just a little movement, that's all.

Honk honk. The car horn interrupted her thoughts. Hannah jumped back, out of Harry's grasp, to see Coco watching them in her old VW Bug.

"I have to go," Hannah mumbled, running towards the car. She climbed in and slammed the door. "Please go quickly."

Chapter 11

Coco reversed away from the bonfire party and had the old car on the road in no time. "Do you want to talk about anything?"

"No."

"Did Harry upset you?"

"No."

"Have you been drinking?"

"No," Hannah shot back, incredulous that she would even ask. Sure, there was alcohol there, but she didn't touch the stuff. "Did you have to come in your pajamas?"

"Why would I change?" Coco asked, equally as incredulous at the question.

"You like embarrassing me, don't you?"

"Only because it's so much fun," Coco joked, trying to lighten the mood. She knew something was wrong with her daughter but trying to unlock that secret was like trying to crack a safe. "I'm really glad

56

you called me to pick you up. I want you to know that no matter what happens, at any time, you can call me and I'll be there for you. I don't care what the situation is."

Hannah looked at her mother, the shadows of the streetlights flickering over her face as she drove. She loved her so much, even if she did wear her pajamas in public. "Thanks, Mom."

"You're welcome, sweetie." She reached over and placed a hand on Hannah's leg, a silent, comforting gesture. They didn't speak again until they were home.

Billy raced up to greet them, jumping all over them like he hadn't seen them for a year. Hannah caught him, lifting the little dog up for a cuddle.

She buried her face against Billy, knowing he would never break her heart. He was the best companion there was, he never asked any questions and thought she was the best person on the planet. If only boys were more like dogs, Hannah thought to herself.

"I'll make you a cup of tea," Coco offered without waiting around for a response. She hurried to the kitchen, leaving Hannah and Billy to cuddle on the lounge.

When she returned with two steaming hot mugs of tea, Coco took her place on the lounge. She sipped, waiting for Hannah to start the conversation.

She didn't have to wait too long. "Are relationships always this hard, Mom?" She continued facing the television as she waited for a reply.

"Relationships are hard work," Coco said gently. "But they can also be absolutely wonderful. When you fall in love with someone, it's like everything in the world has aligned just for you two to be together. It's magical."

"Why doesn't that feeling last?"

"Because the world gets in the way too. If you can still love that person even though the magic has subsided, then you know it's true love."

"So you and Dad weren't in true love then? Is that why he left?" Hannah asked, trying to make sense of it all. There was so much she didn't understand, it sounded like walking through an entire minefield and just waiting for the bombs to explode.

Coco smiled kindly. "We were in true love, but sometimes things happen and people change. Sometimes even love isn't enough. It's a tricky world out there, honey. I'm still trying to make sense of it too."

"Would you let yourself fall in love again?"

"Absolutely. Falling is half the fun. It's the holding on part that's a bit difficult."

Hannah stared into her tea, watching the few stray leaves settle on the bottom. She wondered what a fortune teller would say about the leaves. Did they fall in a good or bad way?

The next day brought no new answers to her problems. It did, however, bring routine. Hannah made it to the shelter just before her shift was about to start, parking her bike and entering like nothing had happened last night. That was the plan – pretend nothing had changed. They didn't have to get inside her head and know the truth.

Jessie, however, had different ideas. "What happened to you last night?" She demanded. A cat was curled up in her arms as she stroked it.

"I, uh, wasn't feeling well so my mom picked me

up."

"And your phone? I guess that was out of reception or credit or something?"

Guilt struck her, she didn't think anyone would miss her. And Harry knew where she had gone, didn't he talk to them at all for the rest of the night? "Sorry, I didn't think to tell you where I was going."

"We looked for you for ages. Vee ended up texting your mom, she was that desperate."

When had Veronica become Vee to Jessie? Hannah wondered, trying not to be annoyed by that little fact. She had bigger issues at that point. "Look, I'm sorry. I promise I won't do it again."

Jessie relaxed a little, releasing her grip on the cat. "You better not. We have to look out for each other, especially at parties. Anything could happen."

"What happened?" Harry asked as he entered through the back door. He didn't see Hannah until he looked up from the dog he was walking. "Oh. Hi."

"Hi," Hannah replied, wishing the ground would open up at her feet and she could fall into an alternate universe where awkward didn't exist.

Harry ushered the dog into his cage and secured the door, earning a pair of sad eyes cast his way from the fluffy animal. "I'll just grab what I need and be outside."

Jessie stood motionless, staring between the two of them, back and forth. "Did something happen between you two? You're both acting especially weird."

Hannah couldn't find any words to say, her mouth was completely frozen in place. Where was that portal when you needed it?

Harry was no help. "Maybe you should ask Hannah, because I have no idea."

The sadness in his voice and the resigned set to his shoulders stabbed Hannah in the heart. She was the reason he wasn't happy and that only made her unhappy too. She thought he sounded like he had given up. Perhaps he had decided she wasn't worth the effort after all? Perhaps she had lost her chance of getting back together with him?

That thought made her impossibly sad, much more so than she had ever expected. It was funny, the way you only really discovered what you wanted when you no longer had it. Hannah suddenly really wanted Harry to try to get back together with her. She wanted those stupid little love notes, the flirting, the cute little glances, she wanted it all. And now she wouldn't get it anymore. Ever.

Harry grabbed the lid of the snake cage closest to the door as Hannah watched on. Jessie went back to tending to the cat, placing her on the bench and brushing her long fur. From the outside, it looked like a normal day. Hannah wished that was the case.

As Harry pulled the lid away from the cage to place it on the bench, he caught the corner, causing the entire cage to topple to the ground. Hannah watched it happen, almost like it was in slow motion. The glass cage, the snake, and everything else went crashing to the ground – right on top of Harry.

She lunged, trying to stop the fall. It was no use, the glass shattered into a thousand pieces with a loud crash. Jessie screamed, grabbing the cat and running out of the room.

"Get the snake before he escapes!" Harry called

out, trying to get out of the glass without causing more damage to himself.

Hannah panicked as she watched the green snake slither toward the door. It took her two seconds to realize Harry was talking to her, that she was the only one who could grab the slimy thing.

"Hannah, quick!"

She didn't have time to dither any longer. She stepped around the mess and made a jump for the snake. She frantically tried to remember what Harry had shown her about picking it up. Something about grabbing the head and then the body?

Fighting all her instincts to let it go, Hannah grabbed the head. The snake objected, trying to get out of her grasp. She held on, picking up the heavy body so it couldn't go anywhere.

Holding the serpent away from herself as far as possible, Hannah had no idea what to do with the thing. She desperately wanted to put it somewhere out of her sight. "What do I do? What do I do? Ew, ew, ew."

"I'll take it," Harry offered, now standing behind her. She eagerly waited until he took the snake from her, unable to move.

Harry placed the snake in a free tank before turning back to the mess on the floor. Hannah was still motionless, not believing she had actually picked up a snake.

"You did really well," Harry mumbled, grabbing a broom.

Hannah picked up the dustpan and pulled the garbage bin closer. "I touched a snake."

He laughed. "You did."

"It didn't bite me."

"George isn't a big biter."

"I picked up a snake," she repeated, wondering if she would be able to do it again. Considering she didn't lose an arm or anything, perhaps she could.

Chapter 12

"You're such a cute little pain in the butt, aren't you?" Hannah cooed, watching the monkey grip her fingers through the cage.

He had recovered well from his injuries, the vet was satisfied he was ready to go home – wherever that was. Nobody had come forward to claim him, despite Cory's attempts to get the word out that he was there.

"Where did you come from? Who owns you?" She asked, wishing the monkey could talk. It would make their lives so much easier if all the animals could tell them where their homes were.

The monkey gave her a meaningful gaze with his big brown eyes. He was still a little groggy with the pain medicine but he seemed alert enough. Hannah had been keeping him company. She figured he must come from somewhere there were a lot of people because when he was lonely he started screeching. The noise agitated all the other animals – especially the dogs. The snakes didn't much care.

Growing hungry, Hannah fished around in her handbag, trying to find the mints she had thrown in there three days ago. It wouldn't be much but it would tide her over for another little while until lunch.

She found the mints and popped one in her mouth. At the same time, she noticed the flyer for the circus. "Clowns are so creepy," she muttered while the happy, heavily made up faces of the clowns stared back at her.

She read through the flyer:

Big Brother's Big Top Circus. Family Fun for all.
Come see the clowns, the trapeze, the animals.
Come one, come all, to the biggest show on earth.

Hannah recalled the last time she had been to a circus. She was only eight years old at the time, her parents were still together, and her grandmother went with them. One of the ponies bit her, a clown sprayed water from a flower on his lapel at her, and the hay made her nose itch.

Among all those not so perfect memories, she could recall that there were a lot of animals travelling with the circus. There was an elephant, a tiger, and a monkey. Hannah looked from the flyer to her little friend, could he be from the circus? They hadn't reported any animals missing that she knew of, but maybe they hadn't noticed?

"Hannah, I need your help," Cory called from reception.

She stuffed the flyer back into her handbag and promised the monkey she would return later for another visit. She found Cory wrangling with a giant spider. It was delivered by a pest control worker in an ice cream container.

"Ugh, spiders now?" Hannah moaned. "Why didn't they just let it go in the woods or something?"

Cory seemed completely unaffected by the creepy crawly – with emphasis on the *creepy*. "He's a Golden Orb spider, not native to this country. If he's released into the wild then he could play havoc with the eco-system."

"What are you going to do with him?"

"Find his owner and return him, just like all the others," Cory replied, mesmerized with the eight legged freak. Even in a sealed container, the spider was too close for Hannah's comfort. It had a gigantic, bulbous body striped yellow and black like a bee. Her skin crawled at the sight of it.

She avoided the creature until lunchtime, finding things to do everywhere else in the shelter. She couldn't wait until Jessie caught a glimpse of the thing, her shrieks would probably be heard right across town. She hoped she would be there to see it.

Hannah finally made it to lunch, sitting outside in the sun under the shade of a tree. She pulled out her homemade sandwich and munched on the peanut butter and jelly. She had to put all images of the giant spider out of her mind in order to be able to eat.

She saw Harry coming her way and inwardly groaned. He was carrying a brown paper bag which sparked her curiosity. He caught up and sat beside her on the grass.

"I got you something," Harry grinned, holding up the bag. Hannah took it reluctantly, despite dying to know what was inside.

She opened the bag and peeked in. It was a perfect pink cupcake with chocolate sprinkles on top. "You got me a cupcake?"

"I know you don't like pink, but you do like strawberry flavor so I thought it might be okay."

The act was sweeter than the sugar in the cupcake. Hannah couldn't help but smile at the gesture. "It's perfect, thank you."

"You're perfect, it's the least I could do."

Right at that moment, Hannah wanted to throw her arms around Harry's neck and cling to him like moss to a rock. She didn't even remember why it was so important to stay away from him. Perhaps he wasn't done with trying to win her back after all?

To stop herself doing something stupid, Hannah changed the subject. "Did you know there is a circus in town?"

"Yeah, out on the Parklands, I've seen the big tent going up."

Hannah pulled the flyer out of her handbag and passed it to him. "They have animals there. I was maybe thinking they might be short a monkey."

Harry nodded eagerly. "Every circus has a monkey, they ride on the elephants, right?"

"I guess so," she giggled at the imagery. The monkey in the circus she had visited didn't ride on the elephant but she had seen it on television and in movies.

"Do you want to check it out after our shift? We could go for a bike ride, you know, like we used to?" He looked so hopeful there was no way Hannah could turn him down. Not after running out on him at the bonfire party. And if meant finding the monkey's rightful home, it would be worth it.

"Sounds like a plan."

His face burst into a smile. "Or a date?"

"It's not a date."

"It could be."

She smiled, shaking her head at his eagerness. He didn't miss any opportunity. "It's not."

Chapter 13

The wind wasn't as warm as it once was, signaling that summer was winding down for the season. Hannah hated the thought of summer ending, but at least that would mean going back to school. She could immerse herself in her schoolwork and not be so obsessed about boys anymore. That was the plan, anyway.

Harry and Hannah pulled up at Alex Park, the largest parklands in all of Mapleton. Instead of the normal grass and open space, a colorful circus tent was erected. Trucks and wagons circled the perimeter, all bearing the logo for the Big Top Circus.

"This thing is huge," Hannah muttered, trying to take in the dizzying colors and canvas building.

"This thing is amazing," Harry corrected her. They jumped off their bikes and left them at the curb to investigate further.

The circus was closed, their first performance wasn't due for another two days. Strong crew were still trying to assemble the few rides they kept outside the tent.

As Hannah walked, she was extra wary of what could jump out of the tent flaps. They were in clown territory now, the frightening creatures could be anywhere. They liked to scare kids, she was sure that was their mission in life.

Harry, on the other hand, seemed to be enjoying every minute of it. His eyes were glued open, held wide in awe of the closed stands and bright posters.

"Once, I went to the circus with my grandpa," Harry started happily, his hands waving around with excitement. "I was picked to be the magician's assistant. He put this hat on my head and then produced a rabbit... on my head! It came out of nowhere."

"That sounds... interesting." She wanted to say disturbing but managed to refrain herself. "You're really into this whole circus thing, aren't you?"

"Yeah, how could you not love all this?"

His enthusiasm was strangely infectious. Hannah found herself unable to come up with one good reason why she shouldn't like being there. She started giggling. "I guess it's hard to not like it."

Harry continued his searching around, his eyes darting all over the place. "I hope there are clowns here somewhere."

"You actually like clowns?"

"They're always happy," he replied, like it should have been the most obvious thing in the world. "Hey, there's some people. They look important, they might be who we need to speak to."

He pointed to a group of three men, all deep in

discussion. The thought of interrupting them filled Hannah's stomach with dread. She refused to move again until two of the men left, leaving only one behind. One she could deal with. She heard the other men call him Boss. They hurried over before he could disappear behind the red canvas flap.

"Kids, you can't be here," he said sternly. His pants were being held up with old fashioned red suspenders, they had to stretch to reach over his belly. When he talked, his stomach jumped up and down. "This is private property. The show doesn't open for two days."

"We're sorry to bother you, sir," Hannah started. She looked at Harry, nodding that he should take over. The man gave her the creeps.

Harry stepped in. "We're from the Mapleton Animal Shelter, we were wondering if you were missing any animals recently?"

The man's entire demeanor changed in the blink of an eye. His scowl turned into a look of disbelief. "You have my animals?"

They exchanged a glance, Hannah hoped they were talking about the same animals. "We've got snakes, spiders, lizards, and a monkey. Are you missing any of those?"

Boss started nodding his head. "Three snakes, an iguana, two frill-necked lizards, five spiders, and a Capuchin monkey. They've all been missing for over a week now."

Hannah did a quick inventory in her head. They had everything except two of the spiders. She shuddered to think where the missing two had ended up. Hopefully nowhere near her house.

"We have most of them," Hannah answered. "How did you lose them in the first place?"

Sadness washed over Boss's face. "We were in the next town over, putting everything away to come here. In the middle of the night, a group of people broke in and let all the animals go. They accused us of mistreating them. We managed to find most of the animals before they could get too far but some of the scamps got away. We've been worried sick about them."

"Why didn't you report it to the police?" Harry asked.

"We did, back in Huntsville. They didn't think it was an important issue so just filed our report. I left some of my crewmembers there to continue the search."

As much as Hannah believed the man was sorry the animals went missing. She was still concerned about why they had been released in the first place. "*Are* you mistreating the animals? Were the group right in their accusations?"

Boss slid his fingers underneath his suspenders, holding them out like it was a habit to keep his hands occupied. "Of course not. We love our animals, they are our first priority in everything we do. Most of them have been rescued from terrible conditions. We give them a second chance at life. If they don't enjoy being in the show, we retire them and they live out their lives with our families back home."

"Why did they accuse you of mistreating them then?"

"Some people see the circus and assume we don't care about the animals. That's true about some, but not us. We never even have wild animals that shouldn't be caged up like lions or elephants. Reptiles, horses, and the one monkey who has been with me since it was born, that's all we have. They're part of the family."

Hannah remembered seeing reports on news programs about animals in the circus. Many groups had been trying to get them banned for years. She agreed with Boss, all wild animals didn't have a place in the circus. However, she included monkeys in that category too. But considering how well looked after the little guy was, she might make an exception this one time. *Just* this one time.

"When can we collect the animals?" Boss asked eagerly. "Everyone is going to be so excited to know they're safe."

"You can come by tomorrow," Harry replied, giving him the address. "Cory is the manager, she'll have some forms for you to sign."

Tears started to well in Boss's eyes. "I'll be counting down the minutes."

Chapter 14

"How do we know he's the real owner?" Hannah asked, eyeing all the snakes and already imagining how great it would be not to have them in the shelter. Some of the dogs she missed when they left, but she definitely didn't have the same attachment to the slithery kind.

"The monkey will recognize him," Harry shrugged.

"So you're relying on a monkey? Just a monkey?"

"How else will we know? It's not like a spider will run toward its owner."

Failing having a better idea, Hannah shut up. The monkey *had* taken a few days to warm up to her, he didn't seem like the kind who would do anything for some attention. It sounded like the monkey was it.

"Where's Jessie?" Hannah asked, realizing she had only seen her when she first arrived and not since.

"She's decided to walk the dogs as far away from here as possible," Harry answered with a cheeky grin.

"She said she'd come back when all the snakes were gone."

Hannah nodded, she never thought she would say it, but Jessie was the smart one. If she had any sense, she would have grabbed the cats and done the same. Instead, she was left to wait and hope all the reptiles stayed away from her.

Boss, who Cory determined was actually named Arthur, arrived shortly afterwards. He didn't come alone. Much to Hannah's horror, he was accompanied by a band of clowns and muscled sideshow men.

It was strange seeing the clowns out of their make-up, it was like seeing a movie actress on the street enjoying a latte. It didn't quite compute.

"Come this way," Harry directed. He led them through to the back area without telling them which animals were suspected to be theirs.

Instantly, the men disbursed. One of the muscled strongmen went to the iguana. "Daisy!" he exclaimed, hugging the glass enclosure.

"Alfred!" A clown cried when he saw the Golden Orb spider. He couldn't wait for permission to open the lid and start letting the creepy crawly walk over his hands. Hannah stayed put by the door, they were too unpredictable to guarantee none of the creatures would get to her.

Arthur looked around frantically. While seeing the reunions brought a smile to his lips, he knew there was something missing. "Where's Bruce? You said you had a Capuchin monkey here."

"We do," Harry replied, nodding towards Hannah. She took her cue and carefully retrieved the monkey. It gripped onto her shoulder, its little fingers holding on like an infant might.

She returned to the room, studying the creature for any sign of recognition. She didn't have to look too hard. The moment the monkey caught a glimpse of Arthur, it shrieked with excitement.

Forgetting all about Hannah, who had tirelessly cared for it for the past few days, Bruce pushed at her to get away and into his owner's embrace.

"Ah, Bruce, thank God you're okay. I've been worried sick about you," Arthur cooed as he cradled the little monkey. They stared into each other's eyes with such love there was no denying that not only did they belong together, but that Bruce couldn't be mistreated.

Harry stood beside Hannah watching the circus troupe get reacquainted with their animals. He leaned over to whisper in her ear. "Need any more proof?"

She shook her head, watching a clown get wrapped up in a snake and chuckling with every moment. "None. There is no way these animals aren't being treated with love. I never thought it was possible for a lizard to be in love with someone."

"Nobody can help who they fall in love with," Harry commented.

Hannah opened her mouth to retort but was interrupted by Arthur. His face beamed with happiness. "I can't thank you kids enough for keeping these guys safe and finding us. I couldn't imagine living without Bruce. My wife on the other hand..."

"It was our pleasure," Hannah replied. Seeing a reunion, whether it was with a fluffy or scaly creature, made her hours of volunteering worthwhile. There was only one other thing that made her feel all warm and fuzzy like that. And she had broken up with him.

"I'd like to give you all passes to the show." Arthur reached into his pocket while juggling the monkey in his other hand. He pulled out a wad of tickets and handed them to Harry. "And I'd like to make a donation to the shelter, something to cover the costs of looking after all our animal family and more."

Cory suddenly appeared at hearing the magic word: *donation*. "We would be more than happy to accept." She escorted him to her office to take care of business.

Harry looked down at the tickets, the bright, garish faces of clowns stared back at him. "This is awesome."

Hannah wasn't so sure. She had seen her fill of clowns and creatures for one summer. "Yeah," she tried to sound enthusiastic. It didn't quite work.

After all the lizards, spiders, snakes, and one monkey were gone, there was only one thing left to do – clean up. Harry, Hannah, and Jessie fell into a quiet rhythm as they dusted, wiped, and hosed down the cages.

It was just starting to get dark when Hannah finally made it home. She was exhausted, but a little bit of adrenalin remained at doing something great.

She thought it was funny how she never felt that kind of a buzz from her schoolwork. Volunteering was so much more satisfying than she had ever imagined it would be. What had begun as something to keep her mom happy had turned into something she never wanted to stop doing. Being at the shelter had changed her life, in more ways than one.

"Big day?" Coco asked as she watched her daughter slide onto a stool at the kitchen bench. Billy was jumping at her feet to be picked up.

"We found the owners of all the creatures."

"That's fantastic. Who was it?"

"A circus." Hannah laughed as her mother raised her eyebrows in surprise. "I know, right? Who would have thought?"

"I'm just glad they all made it home."

"Me too. I'm *really* glad I don't have to touch any more snakes... or lizards. Ugh." She made a face of disgust. Perhaps she would only look after regular pets when she became a vet, nothing of the slithery kind. That seemed feasible.

"At least you've had a summer to remember," Coco said, smiling warmly.

Hannah's mind flashed with all the things she had seen and done all summer long. Her first kiss, her first love, her first pet. Her favorite memory of them all was being drenched by the ocean on her first date with Harry. She had never laughed that hard before.

It was a summer to remember, she didn't want to forget any of it – even the parts that had upset her. Everything was a learning experience. And her greatest lesson of them all was that life couldn't be learned through school textbooks. You had to get out there, in the big bold world, to really live.

Chapter 15

"This is crazy," Hannah grinned as she looked around. She hadn't been excited about going to the circus, but everyone else was going and she didn't want to be left out. So she had put on a dress, a smile, and tagged along. And it had been awesome.

Harry laughed, watching the clowns run around chasing their tiny runaway car. "I know, right?" His enthusiasm was too powerful, part of the reason why Hannah was having such a good time.

Arthur hadn't just given them tickets, he had treated the entire shelter gang like VIP's all night. They had the best seats – front row, centre – endless amounts of food, and the magician had insisted on Cory being his assistant for a trick. The entire night was worth all the fear of caring for the gigantic spiders.

Hannah was so distracted by the clowns that she didn't notice Harry slip away. "Hey, where's Harry gone?" Jessie shrugged, but the smile on her face told her there was something she was hiding. "Jessie, what do you know?"

"Nothing," she giggled.

Hannah turned her attention to Cory. "Did you see where Harry went?"

"He probably went to the bathroom or something," she replied distractedly.

She considered going to look for Harry, but knew there would be no way to find him amongst the hundreds of people at the show. Cory was probably right, he would come back eventually. It wasn't like he'd accidently get swallowed by the boa constrictor or something, right?

With a honk of their horns, the clowns all took their final bow and received a rousing round of applause for their efforts. They didn't seem as scary when performing, like they were in context or something.

The tent went dark as all the lights were turned off momentarily. A spotlight came on, aimed at the performance doors. Harry was never going to find his way back in the darkness. Drum beats started, growing faster and faster until it was almost one constant stream. Hannah could feel her stomach knot with anticipation.

Acrobats dropped from the roof, swinging back and forth as they threw a woman between them. Hannah thought the safety net underneath them didn't appear to be adequate. At any moment she expected one of them to plummet to their death. It was stressful watching.

Through the performance doors, horses with female riders in sparkly costumes started streaming out. The horses went around and around in circles, looping the entire performance centre. It wasn't long before the girls stood up on their steeds, dancing while riding.

Looking closer, not all the riders were female. Hannah spotted Harry amongst them. He wasn't standing on his horse, but riding it with enthusiasm. He was dancing while sitting down, using the same dodgy moves he used on the dance floor.

"It's Harry," Jessie pointed out, grabbing Hannah on the arm to get her attention. Hannah already couldn't take her eyes off him. He looked happier than she had ever seen him.

The horses stopped their routine, all lining up to face the front. Harry was in the middle, his face wide with a grin. All the performers jumped to the ground to stand next to their horse.

The spotlights moved up to the acrobats, still swinging and swaying in the air. The one on the left caught the flying girl and she stood on the swing. The acrobat swung again but there was nothing else to catch. Instead, the other acrobat handed him something.

When he swung back, a big sign was revealed. They each held an end until it was completely open. Hannah quickly read it, fearing it wouldn't stay there for very long. It read:

Harry Loves Hannah Forever

It was the most reckless, stupid, charming, adorable, sweetest thing anyone had ever done for her. The spotlight moved to Hannah, lighting her up for the entire circus to see. She wanted to yell at Harry for embarrassing her at the same time she wanted to cry over how nice it was.

He had done all the routine for her, secretly arranged for the performance and sign, just to surprise her. All so he could win her back?

It was crazy, *he* was crazy, was all Hannah could think. Who did that for someone? It was insane, something that only happened in movies. He had warned her he would do something epic to win her back but she never expected him to join a circus. What on Earth was he thinking?

Through the bright spotlight, Hannah looked down at Harry. All the façade of performing was gone, leaving only the face that she knew so well. His kind blue eyes, his dimple on only one cheek, his hair that fell into his eyes because he always needed a haircut. He was worried, she could tell.

He shouldn't have been. Hannah stood and jumped the barrier separating her from the performance area. The spotlight followed her every move. She ran at him, not stopping until she burst into his arms.

Harry swung her around, over and over again until they were both dizzy and laughing. He let her go, only to cradle her head in both of his hands. "Does this mean I've won you back?"

She nodded, worried she wouldn't be able to say the words without crying.

"I love you, Hannah."

She risked sounding like a blubbering fool. "I love you too. I never stopped."

In front of the entire circus, Hannah reached up and planted her lips on Harry's. A kiss had never felt so good before. It was pure bliss and happiness, promising of nothing but good times ahead.

Butterflies buzzed in her stomach as she remembered her mother's words – falling was one of the best parts. And she would fall for Harry over and over again if necessary.

When they finally parted, Hannah remembered the hundreds of people watching them. She turned around to face her audience, her face burning red as she blushed. Yet instead of shrinking away like she might have done once, she took Harry's hand and they bowed. The crowd erupted into cheering and applause. None more so than Cory and Jessie.

It had been a big summer, and Coco was right when she said it was one to remember. In her head, she would replay it over and over again, probably for the rest of her life. But now all Hannah could think of was that she had a new favorite moment. And it was happening right now.

❧ The End ❧

My Hairy Tails

Many of the animals in this series were inspired by my own pets. I would like to introduce them to you.

TOM (THUMB):

Tom was rescued from the pound after being severely attacked by a group of German Shepherds. He was a Chihuahua cross, and brave enough to take on dogs much bigger than he was.

We had him for over sixteen years before he passed away. He was a loyal and loving friend the entire time. And he always thought he was big enough to take on the big dogs.

Tom was the inspiration for Billy in the series.

(MIGHTY) MAX:

If there was something Max loved, it was food. Once, we made the mistake of leaving an Easter egg on the table within reach. Not ten minutes later, he had eaten the entire thing, leaving nothing but the foil scattered across the floor from one end to the other.

Max made a special guest appearance in A Hairy Tail 3 as Maximus at the animal fashion parade.

SNOOPY (MR MAGOO):

Snoopy was a breath of fresh air, the loopiest little thing there was. He used to let me cradle him like a baby in my arms, always up for a snuggle. He was brave too, if I screamed he would be the first one on the scene and ready to take on the enemy.

We lost Snoopy only last year and the pain is still fresh. Not a day goes past when I don't miss his bright little face begging for food.

ANGEL (PIE):

Angel currently weighs about double what she does in this photograph. She prowls around for food at every opportunity she gets.

Found in her bed, stretched out on her back with her belly in the air, Angel will always take a cuddle and some food (especially the food).

(WILY) WILLOW & SOPHIE (SUE):

Willow loves his bed, curling up in a little ball and snuggling away in the bedroom all day. He has this weird way of jumping down from somewhere, he doesn't exactly jump, just lets himself fall. He's weird, he fits in well with the rest of the family.

Sophie is my best friend and office assistant. She is always at my feet, no matter where I am or what I am doing. She loves her special bed under my computer and is constantly telling me what to do. She is the boss, definitely not me.

A Message From the Author:

I hope you enjoyed the Hairy Tails series as much as I did writing them. While the adventures of Hannah and Harry were fun to write, there was a message I wanted to get across.

No, it's not that animals are cute, we know that already. I wanted people to understand how important it is that mistreated, abandoned, and unwanted animals have a place to be cared for. Every animal deserves to be loved, cared for, and kept safe – just like every human.

If it wasn't for the extraordinary work that shelters do around the world, there would be no-one to give animals a voice to be heard. The people that run these places and generously volunteer their time are true super heroes.

I urge everyone to play their part. Donate a can of food, a blanket, some time. Together, wonderful things can be accomplished to make the world a better place. It doesn't take much.

And you never know, maybe your Hannah, Harry, or Jessie is out there waiting to meet you.

Stay cool, pups.

xoxo Jamie

About The Author

Jamie Campbell grew up in the New South Wales
town of Port Macquarie as the youngest of six
children. A qualified Chartered Accountant, she now
resides on the Gold Coast in Queensland, Australia.

Writing since she could hold a pencil, Jamie's passion
for storytelling and wild imagination were often a
cause for concern with her school teachers. Now that
imagination is used for good instead of mischief.

Visit www.jamiecampbell.com.au now for exclusive
website only content.

Made in the USA
Middletown, DE
22 October 2022